Yours Truly, Love, Janie

Ann Reit

SCHOLASTIC INC.
New York Toronto London Auckland Sydney

For everyone who lived in 5A —

Cover photo by Owen Brown

ISBN 0-590-40648-5

Copyright © 1981 by Ann Reit. All rights reserved. Published by Scholastic Inc.

12 11 10 9 8 7 6 5 4 3 2 1   6 7 8 9/8 0 1/9

Printed in the U.S.A.   06

Yours Truly, Love, Janie

A Wildfire Book

WILDFIRE TITLES

CHAPTER I _____

Everybody says sixteen is a wonderful age to be. But I've just begun to realize that the everybodies who say this have forgotten what it's like to be sixteen. Or maybe they never were the kind of sixteen I am.

I know I have all kinds of good things going for me, and I know I'm one of the fortunate girls in this world. But I have this feeling of *restlessness*. I'm always waiting for *something* to happen.

I live in a nice, respectable suburb of New York City, so I have the excitement of going to the city and the cozy feeling of living in a small town. My mother is pretty and fun and owns a small book and gift shop in town. When disaster strikes and I run out of money or I've locked myself out of the house, all I

1

have to do is bike to her store and throw myself on her mercy. She isn't always exactly delighted to see me at times like that, but if I'm lucky and she has a customer, I don't get lectured on: "Responsibility is the first step toward maturity."

My father commutes into the city every day. I'm not sure exactly what benefits I get from his being a lawyer, outside of food and shelter, but I guess if I ever get arrested, I'll know. He's getting a little paunchy and his hair is thinning on top, but I like it. It makes him look "fatherly." When he's home he is usually buried behind legal papers, but anytime I've really needed him, he's been there. Mom, too. They try very hard to be modern and fair, but they can also say, "Absolutely no," when necessary. I have to admit, though I protest loudly when this happens, I really like it. It makes me feel ... protected, I guess.

My sister, Melanie, is twenty and away at college. (My mother was reading *Gone with the Wind* when she was pregnant. She couldn't quite bring herself to call her Scarlett, so she settled for Melanie.) Melanie and I really get along quite well. There are the usual sisterly battles, but underneath the surface hatred we like each other. The only thing I can't stand about her is that she has naturally curly, blonde hair.

But to tell the truth, I even like the way I *look*. I'm not gorgeous or anything like that, but I am kind of pretty. I'm what you call the delicate type, small and slim (but with enough curves in the right places so that you know I'm a girl). I have long, straight, brown hair (now you see why I hate Melanie) and brown eyes that people say show whatever I'm feeling. Most teenage girls are always saying, "I can't *stand* the way I look." But I feel, all things considered, I've done okay.

And then there is Peter. Peter Ingersoll and I have been going together for sixteen years. I think the day I was born (he's two years older than I), he walked over and said, "Save the Junior Prom for me." Peter is good-looking, tall, blonde, with bright blue eyes. He's smart. He's a star basketball player. He loves me. He's dependable. But I think I know everything about him; there's nothing he could do or say that would surprise me. I feel warm and friendly and secure when he kisses me . . . and that's not the way I want to feel. There are no rockets or bells or electric shocks. So I guess he's why I always feel this restlessness.

I once read about a girl whose lover's eyes reflected "pools of mystery." I keep looking for some pools in Peter's eyes, but all I see is open, honest blue. I often think maybe he has some great tragic secret in his past that I don't know about. But the only tragic secret in his past is the first year he went to sleep-away camp, when he was eight, and he was so lonesome his parents had to take him home. That's hardly fuel for a romantic novel. I guess I just want him *different*. Or more honestly, I want to feel differently about him ... excited and tense.

"Hey, Janie, it's me. Are you upstairs?" I heard the front door slam and Tina's voice all at the same time.

"Come on up. I'm in my room."

When Tina appeared in my door, I looked up from my bed where I was lying and felt the same moment of pleasure I always feel when I see her. Tina Warrens is my best friend, and she is and looks special. It isn't just that she's five eight and holds herself tall and straight, loving every inch of her height. Or that her pencil slimness makes an old, torn shirt on her look like a St. Laurent design. Or that her short, sleek, light-brown hair and green eyes are just right for her face. It's all of these things put together ... and the way she doesn't pay any attention to any of them.

"What are you doing?" she asked.

"Brooding," I told her with a shrug.

"Do you want me to ask what about, or not?" She sat down on the bed and took an apple I was eating out of my hand.

"I want you to ask," I said, taking the apple back.

"Okay, what about?" she asked dutifully.

"Well ... do you ever say to yourself, 'Is this all there is to life?' "

She thought for a moment and then answered, "Only when it's my turn to clean the bathroom."

4

"Very funny," I muttered, turning on my side.

She put her hand on my shoulder gently. "You're serious?"

I turned back to her and saw the concern in her green eyes. "Well, not serious to the death, but serious enough."

Tina shook her head. "I always think of you as Janie Downs, the girl who has it made. You know, pretty, smart, great parents, good-enough sister, wonderful boyfriend."

Jasmine, my Siamese cat, who was sitting on my stomach, let out a loud meow, as only a Siamese can, at that moment. Tina nodded at her and said, "Sorry about that. *And* exceptional cat."

We laughed, and I felt strangely embarrassed. "Maybe I've lost my mind. Or I'm just the most selfish girl in all of New York State."

Tina looked puzzled. "It's not either of those, but I can't think of anything to say to help you. I guess it's just 'our age.'"

I jumped up from the bed. "Yeah, you're right. And I'm not going to live to be any older if I don't get downstairs and put the potatoes in to bake. My parents will be home soon."

As we walked downstairs Tina said, "Why don't you come over tonight. We'll watch TV and eat everything in the house."

"Gee, I'd love to, but Peter is coming over to help me with my Latin. I can't conjugate

5

anything. I don't know, but Latin is just Greek to me."

Tina made a face and pushed me into the kitchen.

"What are you doing, playing little girl and letting big, smart man help you?"

I looked at her with astonishment. "Are you kidding? It's strictly a reciprocal arrangement. He can't even add the seven points to the score when he makes a basket. I help him with math and he helps me with Latin."

"Okay, okay," Tina said as she went out the front door. "I'll see you tomorrow."

While I was standing in the sparkling, yellow kitchen, scrubbing the potatoes as if they had some contagious disease, I looked out of the window over the sink. It was dark, but I could see the remnants of the last, heavy March snowfall in our backyard. I could also see the reflection of my face in the window glass. I stuck my tongue out at the girl I saw and said, *"Idiot!"*

CHAPTER II_____

Dinnertime is special in my family. It is the only time of the day when everybody is together in the same place, so we all try to be agreeable. We don't always succeed, but we try. I think my mother unconsciously made the dining room especially pretty. The flowered wallpaper made the room cheerful and bright, and the polished, dark furniture gave it warmth. When Mother lit candles on the table, everything seemed almost festive, even though there were just the three of us. The dining room always made me feel safe and secure, as if nothing could hurt me as long as I stayed within its quiet walls.

That night, Mother was telling us about a crazy customer she had had that day when Peter appeared in the doorway. He looked so handsome in jeans and a pale blue, soft sweater. It made his eyes brilliant and his hair gold in the candlelight. I waited to see if my heart would beat just a little bit faster, but it didn't. I *liked* his being there, but it didn't make everything suddenly seem magical. Peter never hid his feelings about me from my parents, so he came over to my chair and put a kiss on the top of my head.

"Pull a chair over, Pete," Mother said. She liked him, both my parents did. He was part of the family, almost. I think they felt, and they were right, that Peter was a boy they could trust their "little girl" with. Maybe that's why I felt the way I did. Not that I wanted him to attack me. I just felt it never even *occurred* to him.

We then started the traditional little game that was played whenever Peter arrived at dessert time, which he always did. Mother said, "Like some dessert?"

It was chocolate pudding that night, with real whipped cream. I am happy to say that my mother, though she feels good nutrition is important, is not one of those people who thinks that eating chocolate pudding indicates as strong a death wish as driving a car with one wheel missing.

Peter looked at the pudding casually and answered, "I don't know. I just had dessert at home."

"Oh, just a small portion," my father coaxed.

"Well, just a little." We all laughed as Peter reached for the dish.

I felt like a louse, but I just wished he'd say, *No*, mean it, and not take any. Just for a change.

I noticed my mother looking at Peter wistfully, as he dumped a huge spoonful of whipped cream on his huge dish of pudding. "Why didn't they have boys around that looked like you when *I* was a girl?"

My father looked up and held his spoon suspended in midair. "Fran, *I* was around when you were a girl."

"Jack, darling, I was out of college when we met. I mean when I was a *girl*, young. Like Janie, before the age of real sense."

"You mean you think I'm senseless?"

"Janie, no. I don't mean that at all. You know I don't. I only mean you aren't . . . well, you aren't . . ."

I just kept staring at her.

She came over and kissed me. "I'm sorry, honey. I am. I don't know what I mean. Forgive?"

I reached up and touched her short, blonde hair (like Melanie's) and wanted to say something to erase the concern in her big brown eyes (like mine).

"You knew not what you were saying," I said loftily. "I forgive you."

Peter finished the last speck of his pudding, came over to me, and took my hand. "It's Latin time. Enough of this happiness."

We went into the small den we have and I started to walk over to the table where I'd put my Latin books. Peter stopped and led me to the soft, beige couch that was in a dimly lit corner. "A little more happiness first."

He sat down and pulled me next to him. I could smell the very faint odor of after-shave lotion and the cold winter air that was still in his hair, and the just plain Peter smell of soap and, I guess, healthiness. I would know Peter in the darkest cave in the world, just from these lovely, familiar odors. When he took me in his arms, I felt as if I were floating in warm, soft water, totally relaxed and cozy and safe. But I wanted to feel as if I were in the ocean, gliding on high, exhilarating waves. I felt guilty because Peter was so dear, and angry because he was so familiar. He wound his hand through my hair and whispered, "I love you, Jane."

The only time he called me Jane was when he was loving me, never when he was angry or playful. The sound of my name, *Jane*, somehow made me want to cry. I reached up and touched his face, "You are the best in the world, Peter Ingersoll. Too good for me, I think."

He pulled my hair. "You're right. But I've decided to put up with your shortcomings, like being a dunce in Latin, which we are now going to study."

We sat at the bridge table piled with Latin

books and papers, and Peter said, "Conjugate the verb *amare*."

I began to drone, "*Amo, amas, amat, am* . . . How come you picked the verb *to love*?"

Peter laughed. "I want you to be able to tell me you love me in every language, even dead ones."

"That reminds me. I've got a great idea for what we can go as to Kathy's party Saturday night."

"Go as?" Peter looked puzzled.

"Peter, I *told* you. It's a come-as-your favorite-fictional-character party. And I think we should go as Romeo and Juliet." He looked very uninterested. "I'll be Juliet," I said brightly, expecting a big yak from Peter.

"Oh, no. We are not going as Romeo and Juliet. At least I'm not going as Romeo."

"Why not?" I asked with annoyance. "I want to wear one of those beautiful, flowing dresses and a little cap. And you'd look great as Romeo. You can show off your legs."

"Nope. They were both ridiculous. Dumb kids who didn't have a brain between them."

I couldn't believe what he was saying. "They were the greatest lovers of all time."

"Maybe, but dumb ones. *She* takes some stuff that makes her look dead. Crazy! Then *he* kills himself because he *thinks* she's dead. Serves him right for getting involved with a fourteen-year-old."

"*Peter*! He couldn't bear to live without her."

He went on looking arrogant and smug. "Then *she* wakes up and sees him dead, and she really finishes herself off. Now, why? She was just a kid, had it all ahead of her."

I had gotten up and was furiously putting my books together. "Because she couldn't bear to live without him. You wouldn't understand that."

"You bet I wouldn't understand it. Janie, what are you doing? We haven't even begun to study. Your exam is Tuesday and Tuesday is tomorrow."

I looked at him with total disgust and said with what I thought was mature dignity, "I don't care to study with anyone as insensitive and cold-hearted as you. What could I possibly learn? I'm going upstairs."

Peter laughed and kissed my cheek lightly. "Okay, babe. I'll see you tomorrow."

As he left the room, I yelled after him angrily, "And *don't* call me *babe*."

CHAPTER III_____

When I woke up the next morning, I lay in bed without moving, thinking about the night before. I'd been hard on Peter and he was so accepting of me and all my moods, and I sure was having a lot of them lately. I looked at the window that was etched with ice and the curtains that were moving very slightly. Mother and I had really done a job on the room after she had looked at it a year ago and said, "Something has to change. It looks as if you were still ten years old."

She had pulled the white, organdy curtains off the window and to my horror dyed them brown. When I saw her lower them into the water, I yelled, "Brown? Yuch."

She'd looked up and said firmly, "Don't

'yuch' until you see the finished job." And she was right.

We had painted the walls the very palest of yellows, bought a wildly colored flowered spread for the maple bed, and a shaggy, beige rug for the floor. Mother found an old dressing table in a thrift shop and made a skirt out of another pair of dyed-brown curtains. My comfortable easy chair I refused to let her touch, loving every time I sat in it and sank right to the floor. I painted my desk to match the walls, hung up some posters and Van Gogh prints, and felt as if I had a new nest.

But this morning I was too uneasy to feel the usual contentment when I looked around my room. By lunchtime, I had worked myself up to a good case of *Something has to happen* again.

When I came into the cafeteria, Tina and Kathy Fairchild were already at the table we always shared. Kathy raised her eyebrows at my tray of cottage cheese and fruit.

"What's with you?" she asked, her huge brown eyes in her chocolate-colored face gazing at the cheese.

"I've decided to come to your party as Juliet, and I figure she was frail and ethereal. So I'm on the cottage cheese bit for the rest of the week."

Tina eyed me and said, "You look frail enough to me." She lifted her fork and was about to eat when she noticed Kathy and me staring at her plate.

14

"What is *that*?" I motioned to a glutinous mound next to her hamburger.

Tina looked at me. "What do you mean, '*What is that*?' It's rice."

Kathy leaned over and pushed some of it around with her fork. "It's green rice!"

Tina casually put a forkful in her mouth while we watched with fascination. "Peas! Could have fooled me."

We all laughed and went back to eating. Tina examined me closely and said, "Speaking of green, you don't look so great today. What's up?"

"Nothing really." But then I launched into a detailed description of the argument Peter and I had had the night before.

Tina shook her head. "Let's face it, boys are just not as romantic as girls. At least not most of the time. You have to adjust to it."

Kathy agreed. "I know how you feel. Tommy is the same, but like Tina says, you have to adjust. You're not going to change him."

I stared at a piece of orange as if I'd never seen one before and said in a low voice, "I just wish he was a little different. You know, dashing. I wish I didn't know him so well."

The three of us sat silently for a moment and then I stood up. "I've got to get a book from the library. Anyone want to come to my house after school?"

Kathy moved her tongue around her mouth

and shuddered. "I've got a dentist appointment. Lost a filling."

"I'll be there," Tina said. "I have to stop in Mr. Nesbit's office for a short conference, so I'll be a little late."

"See you later, then." I left them, knowing they were going to discuss my "state of mind," but I loved them both for caring.

By the time I got home after school I was feeling good again. I built a fire in the fireplace in the living room and got out fruit and pretzels and Cokes for Tina and me. Taking a pile of magazines from the coffee table next to the couch, I sat in front of the fire, reading with Jasmine in my lap. I particularly liked looking at the Personal column in *East Coast* magazine. The ads about movers called *Shirley and Daughters,* and vacations in Tahiti, and apartments in Paris for exchange, and people looking for companions entranced me. And then I saw it. The words leaped off the page at me:

> GOOD-LOOKING COWBOY: sensitive, intelligent, 21 years old, wishes to correspond with equally understanding, sophisticated city girl. Write Box 64J, Trentville, Wyoming.

I read the little ad over and over again. I could see Box 64J as if he were in the room. He was *very* tall and *very* slim, and his skin was burned a ruddy tan by the blazing Wyoming sun. His hair was a deep reddish-brown, and his eyes were almost black, reflecting deep pools of mystery and sensitivity. He had a crooked smile that tried to hide, but didn't, the secret tragedy in his past. He wore tight jeans and a plaid, flannel shirt with a yellow scarf knotted around his throat. His cowboy boots came almost up to his knees and a tan cowboy hat was pushed to the back of his head.

I saw him on his gleaming brown horse, riding over the plains or prairie or range or wherever cowboys rode. I really had no knowledge of what a cowboy *did*, so it was a little hard for me to see Box 64J in action. But I knew this was the *something* I had been waiting for.

I ran over to the desk in the corner of the room and grabbed a pad and pencil. I settled myself on the big, comfortable couch near the fire and thought for a while. Then I wrote:

Dear Box 64J,

I saw your ad in *East Coast* magazine and think I am very likely the girl you are looking for. I don't *quite* live in the city, but I am only thirty minutes away, and, of course, I spend most of my time there.

In my mind, sophistication is really how one views and feels about life. Not that experience isn't important, of course, but it is possible to have a

sophisticated *heart*, which I naturally
have, and you must have, even in Wyoming.

I am sensitive and understanding and
have found lately that *that* is hard to
find in other people.

I am not quite as old as you are. I'm
a student, but I'm sure we have a great
deal to share with each other, because
you sound so interesting and mature.

I would very much like to correspond
with you and know all about you, and
hope you will answer this letter quickly.

Yours truly,
Janie

P.S. I'm not giving you my last name
until we know each other a little better.
After all, I don't even know your *first*
name.

J.

"What are you writing?" Tina asked as she
collapsed on the couch.

I looked up startled. "I didn't even hear
you come in."

"I know. You were so involved in what
you're doing. I keep telling you to keep the
door locked when you're alone. Genghis Khan
and his whole band could come in and you
wouldn't know it. What are you writing?"

With some misgivings I showed Tina the
ad in *East Coast*. She read it silently until
she repeated aloud, " 'Wishes to correspond

with sophisticated city girl.' Do you know any sophisticated city girls?"

I held up the pad timidly and smiled as charmingly as I could. Tina took it and read for a minute.

"You're crazy," she said. "Totally deranged."

I reached out and tried to grab the pad from her hand, but she jumped up and backed away from me.

"Honestly, Janie, what do you mean you spend most of your time in the city? You go to New York maybe once a month."

I unsuccessfully grabbed for the pad again. "Sometimes twice," I said angrily.

Tina went on. " *'Sophistication is really how one views and feels about life.'* What does *that* mean?"

"I haven't decided yet. But you have to admit it sounds good."

Tina sat down next to me again. "Janie, you don't have a sophisticated heart. You have a beautiful, sixteen-year-old one."

"Tina, this is the something I've been waiting for. I know it."

Tina ignored me completely and looked at my letter again. " *'I am not quite as old as you are.'* That's for sure." Then she snorted. " *'I am a student.'* You make it sound as if you're studying to be a brain surgeon."

"I'm going to send the letter, Tina. No matter what you say."

Tina sighed and shook her head. "What do you have in common with a cowboy? What are the two of you, if he answers, going to write about?"

I pulled my legs up to my chest, put my head on my knees, and stared into the fire. "I don't know. We'll talk about *life*, and understanding, and sensitivity."

"Oh, heavens." Tina jumped up again and started pacing around the room. "He could even be Jack the Ripper. You don't know."

I looked at her with disgust. "What would Jack the Ripper be doing taking an ad in a personal column in *East Coast*?"

Tina wheeled around triumphantly. "He'd be trying to entice dumb, sixteen-year-old girls like you."

Now *I* snorted. "You know that's not true. He's probably just a lonesome cowboy who wants some company."

"Now you sound like Kenny Rogers. You'll burst into song any minute."

Tina looked at me from where she was standing across the room. She walked over to the couch and sat next to me, gazing silently into the fire. We sat that way for a few minutes. Then she said in a very low voice, "What do you suppose he looks like?"

We grabbed each other and rocked back and forth with laughter, until I was on the floor holding my stomach. Tina suddenly stopped laughing and asked, "Are you going to tell your parents?"

I stopped laughing, too. "Well, not right away. I mean, not that they would object, but . . ." The sentence ended in no tone of assurance.

"Then how are you going to get his letters? He can't write here, if you don't want them to find out. And we both know they wouldn't exactly leap with joy about your writing to a cowboy in Wyoming."

I twisted a long strand of hair around my finger and said, "I'll just have to get a box at the post office like 64J has."

Tina stood up, getting ready to leave. "This is getting more complicated. And what about Peter?"

I walked Tina to the front door and answered with annoyance. "What *about* Peter? I'm not getting married. I'm just writing a letter."

"Yeah. Yeah," Tina said. She leaned over and kissed me on the cheek. "Good luck."

Somehow, I got through the rest of the day and evening, doing all the things that had to be done. I helped with dinner, talked with my parents while we ate, watched a little TV with them, and then, finally, went up to my room. I sat at my desk and carefully copied the letter to Box 64J on my best stationery. I planned to go to the post office the next day after school and get a box, include the number in my letter to 64J, and then mail it. I folded the original letter, hastily written on the pad, and put it in a desk drawer. I knew I'd probably read it over a hundred times.

When I got into bed, I lay on my back and

wondered what 64J was doing that very minute. Maybe sleeping around the campfire, after a busy day of roping and branding. I smiled as I watched shadows from the streetlights moving over the ceiling, and finally I fell asleep.

CHAPTER IV_____

The next morning when I left the house to go to school, Peter was waiting for me. He put an arm over my shoulders as we walked along and said apologetically, "Look, I hope you understand about the Romeo bit. I mean it just isn't for me."

"That's okay. I guess you have to express yourself, but *I'm* going as Juliet."

He gave me a quick hug and whispered in my ear, "You'll be a beautiful Juliet." Then he stopped in front of me and said, "Just to show you I'm not without a literary side, and still hold to my convictions, I've decided to go as Robinson Crusoe."

"Robinson Crusoe," I shouted. "That's sure romantic!"

"I didn't say romantic, I said literary,"

Peter shouted back. Then he stopped walking and put both hands on my shoulders. "Look, Janie, let's not fight about this. It's stupid."

"I'm sorry, Pete. You're right. You'll be a wonderful Robinson Crusoe."

Peter put his arm back around me. "How about a bike ride after school?"

The only thing I wanted to do after school was get to the post office, rent a box, and mail my letter to 64J. I cleared my throat nervously and said, "I'd love to, but I promised Tina I'd go shopping with her. You understand."

"Sure, sure. It's okay." We had reached school and went in different directions to our first class. As we separated, Peter yelled after me, "I'll call you tonight."

I walked to my class in a daze. It was the first time I had ever lied to Peter. Little, unimportant, white lies once in a while, but this was different. This was lying because I didn't want him to know about 64J. I felt awash with guilt, and then I got angry. I wasn't tied to Peter, after all. I could write to anyone I wanted to. I went into my English class, slammed my books on the desk, and hurled myself into my seat. Kathy, who sat in front of me, turned around. "You're in a dandy mood, I see."

"Don't even talk to me. I'll snap at you and hate myself."

Just then Ms. Evans came in and Kathy turned back with a laugh. "You don't scare me."

24

I went through the day feeling like I was under water. I was just existing until I could get to the post office. At lunch I realized I was too nervous to go alone, and Tina agreed to meet me after school and hold my hand.

As we walked into the post office Tina said, "Are you sure you want to go through with this?"

"Of course, I'm sure. Why wouldn't I be sure?" I went to a window and practically whispered to the woman behind it, "I want to rent a post office box."

She leaned forward. "I can't hear you."

I repeated louder and with more assurance, "I want to rent a post office box."

The woman looked at me and asked, "Are you eighteen? You have to be eighteen."

Tina and I exchanged glances. "I just want a box," I said, "not a wedding license."

The woman looked very bored. "You *have* to be eighteen."

"I am eighteen. I just look younger. It's my genes. My mother looks younger and my grandmother, why she . . ."

"Okay, okay. Just fill this out." The woman pushed a form toward me. I took it, answered the questions, and returned it to her.

"That will be ten dollars."

I stared at her stupidly. "Ten dollars?"

"Yeah, ten dollars for six months. That's the charge. You didn't think it was *free*?"

"Of course not," I said, pulling Tina away from the window.

I went through my bag frantically and

pulled out seven dollars. "I've got seven dollars that I was going to buy the new Donna Summer record with," I whispered to Tina. "How much have you got?"

Tina unhappily gave me the three dollars I needed.

"I'm going to return it to you," I said with annoyance.

She made a face. "I just don't think the lonesome cowboy is worth ten dollars . . . three of them mine."

"Well I do," and I handed the money over to the woman behind the window.

On the way home I put my arm through Tina's and promised, "I'm not going to even give him another thought until the letter comes, and I don't even *really* care if he writes or not."

"Ho-ho," Tina said.

Ignoring her, I changed the subject. "What are you going to Kathy's party as?"

"I've decided on Little Red Riding Hood."

"You're joking! You want to go as a nursery rhyme character? That's really glamorous. Why did you pick her?"

"I thought I could put a cute costume together," Tina said, "and I'd kind of like to meet a wolf."

"You have a point there," I admitted. "As for me, I've done it again. Left everything for the last minute. I want to be an ethereal, gorgeous Juliet in a long, flowing gown, and I don't have a long, flowing gown."

"Your mother will do something," Tina tried to reassure me.

"Yeah, have a fit."

That night at dinner I finally brought the subject around to the party. "Did I tell you? I'm going to Kathy's party as Juliet."

"You'll be beautiful," Dad beamed.

My mother smiled. "You *will* look lovely. What are you going to wear?"

"Well, that's the problem. I haven't really done anything about that."

Mother looked at me with amazement. "It's Wednesday, the party is Saturday, and you haven't done anything about that yet? Janie, you really can be irresponsible."

I leaned back in my chair and decided to just wait out the lecture.

"I mean, you want to be treated like an adult and then you do something totally childish. Do you have any idea of what you want to wear?"

"Sure I do, something white and flowing and graceful and ..."

Mother pushed her coffee cup away from her and looked at me. "And I suppose I'm expected to just dream up the perfect costume. Well, it's just too much to expect. For once you'll have ..."

She suddenly stopped and stood up. Taking my hand, she pulled me along with her. "Come with me. You are the luckiest girl in the world to have a wonderful mother like me."

27

I followed her up the stairs and into her bedroom, wondering what she had in mind. When we went into the room I smelled the faint odor of Chanel No. 5, which mother wore most of the time. It was delicate and kind of haunting and it always said to me, *Mother has been here.*

She disappeared in her closet, and I heard grunts and sounds of exasperation until finally she came out holding a hanger covered by a long, white sheet.

"Very attractive," I said.

"Take off the sheet," she instructed, "and don't be a smartie."

I lifted the sheet from the hanger and my mouth fell open with wonder. Cascading from the velvet hanger was the loveliest dress I had ever seen. It was white chiffon with a snug, pleated bodice that fell from two narrow straps. The skirt was yards and yards of swirling chiffon, and around the waist was a girdle of very loosely crocheted, gold metallic thread.

"Mother, it's beautiful. Where did you get it?"

My mother took the dress and gave it to me. "Put it on and let's see how it looks."

I took off my sweater and jeans and slipped the dress over my head. When I looked in the mirror I saw a girl I had never seen before. The swirling, white chiffon and shining gold girdle made me truly look like a possible Juliet. "Oh, Mother," I said softly.

She sat back on the bed and just stared at me. Then she got up, took her comb from the dresser, and pulled large strands of hair on either side of my face to the back of my head. She clipped the hair in place and stood back. "You're really lovely."

By drawing back my hair, my cheekbones looked higher and more pronounced and my eyes looked bigger. My whole face had a more delicate, softer look. Mother said, "Melanie is coming home for the weekend. I'm sure she'll lend you her white evening bag."

"I didn't know Melanie was coming."

"She called this afternoon and told me."

I looked down at my feet and pointed to the dirty, white sneakers poking out from under the chiffon hem. "Do you suppose Juliet wore these?"

Mother laughed. "Not unless she was running in the Verona marathon. You'll have to get shoes . . . those little, white, flat ballet slippers would be perfect."

I sat down on the bed next to my mother and asked, "When did you get the dress?"

She smiled in a very girlish way. "I got it for a New York University ball, when I was seventeen. It was my first *real* evening dress. You know, something that wasn't just a long skirt and blouse."

Mother was leaning against the headboard of her bed and I curled up next to her. "Did you have a good time?"

She put her arm around me and rested her

cheek on the top of my head and laughed. "I had a *terrible* time."

I sat back and stared at her. "Why?" I asked with surprise.

"Well, I went with a boy named Teddy Zenberg. Teddy was a dear boy, but I just *liked* him. He didn't really appeal to me. I remember looking at all the other couples at the dance and they all seemed to be in love. You know, they danced all wrapped around each other, gazing into each other's eyes. I felt so jealous and left out, because I wanted to be in love with Teddy, with anyone, and I wasn't. Dumb, wasn't it? I ruined the evening for myself."

I put my hand on Mother's arm and said, "I don't think it was dumb. I know what you felt."

Then I quickly changed the subject. "Mom, Juliet wouldn't have worn a dress with spaghetti straps, would she?"

"No, you're right. But if you wear that sheer white blouse with the long, loose sleeves under the dress, it will look lovely . . . real Juliet." Then she smiled in a funny way, and she went to the bottom drawer in her bureau and took out a small, tissue-paper-wrapped package and handed it to me.

I opened it carefully and lifted out a small skull cap made of the same gold thread as the girdle on the dress. I let out a cry of delight and put it on the back of my head. "A real

Juliet cap. Oh, Mom, I love you." I threw myself into her arms and she hugged me close.

"I must admit, at times like this I know I
was right I decided to have daughters."

CHAPTER V_____

During the next few days a part of me seemed to always be with my letter to 64J. Every few hours I refigured when would be the soonest I could get an answer. I had mailed it Wednesday. He couldn't possibly get it before Saturday and even if he answered immediately and mailed it immediately, I couldn't really hear from him until the following Wednesday. I had to restrain myself from going to my mailbox on Thursday and Friday. Or rather, Tina restrained me.

"Are you bonkers? You know you couldn't have an answer the day after you wrote. What's with you?"

I laughed ashamedly. "I know. I know. I think I'm losing my mind."

I felt strung up all the time; even Melanie noticed and said to me Friday night, "Are you okay?"

"Of course, I'm okay," I said. "Why do you ask?"

She shrugged. "You just seem funny . . . different."

Saturday night when Peter picked me up for Kathy's party, I felt like I guess people feel when they've had a few drinks. I was giddy and light-headed, and nothing seemed real. Peter looked adorable as Robinson Crusoe. He had put that sun tan stuff on his face and had added a short, false beard. He wore cut-off jeans and a torn white shirt, topped by a tattered straw hat. When he saw me, he really took off. "Wow. If Juliet looked like you I can understand Romeo being a nut."

While we drove to Kathy's house, Peter rambled on about the last game, school, the party, everything. But my mind was thousands of miles away, because I was sure my cowboy had gotten the letter *that day*. It was hard to think of anything else.

When we got to the party, I was distracted for a little while, looking at everyone's costumes. Kathy was absolutely beautiful as the Cathy from *Wuthering Heights*. She wore a white peasant blouse and a full, colorful skirt, and was barefoot. And Tommy was Heathcliff, brooding and sullen, which was hard for him since he was one of the most cheerful people I knew. Tina was the sexiest Red Riding Hood one could imagine. She had on a red miniskirt and white blouse, and red tights, and she had thrown a red cape over her shoulders. Everytime I saw her she was surrounded by all of Filby's wolves.

But once I had looked at the twenty kids who were at the party, and laughed, and tried to guess who everyone was, and once they had looked at me, I drifted back into my cowboy dreams. I hardly heard what anyone said to me, and it was almost impossible for me to carry on a conversation, intelligent or otherwise. When I saw Peter looking at me in a strange way, I went to the other extreme and laughed too loud, and talked too much, and was just plain stupid. But how could I be anything but, when I was totally involved with a letter and a man across the country.

When Peter and I were dancing, he said, "What's with you tonight?"

I pretended I didn't have the vaguest idea what he was talking about. "What do you mean by that? Nothing's with me tonight."

"Well, you're acting very strange. One minute you're not with it at all, and the next you're too with it."

I threw my arms around his neck and danced very close to him, thinking it would distract him. "Oh, Pete, you're imagining things," I said, looking up into his eyes as innocently as I could. They were the blue eyes I knew too well, nothing mysterious in them, nothing hidden.

He pulled me closer to him and said, "Well, maybe I am." When he finally took me home,

I didn't ask him to come in so we could have a little while together cuddling in the living room, which I always did.

"I'm awfully tired, Peter," I said on my doorstep. "Do you mind . . . ?"

He looked hurt but said, "Sure, I know. It's late." He kissed me lightly on the mouth and ran back to his car. "I'll call you tomorrow."

I went up to my room and just lay on my bed with the clouds of white chiffon around me. I thought about the cowboy, and Peter, and felt very confused. Peter had accepted my brush-off so passively. There was a soft knock on my door and Melanie asked, "Are you there?"

I sat up and busily started taking the cap and barrettes from my hair. "Sure, come in."

Melanie sat on my bed and watched me taking off the dress. "You look super."

Actually, Mellie was the one who looked super all the time, even with all her makeup off. Her blonde hair curled around her face, and she had almond-shaped eyes that changed from blue to green, depending on what she was wearing. At that moment she had on a pale blue, quilted robe, so her eyes were blue. Her face was scrubbed and shining and her skin was rosy. Mellie was one of those good people who always washed her face and brushed her hair and teeth before she went to bed. Some nights I tended to be the slob type, and if I was too tired I'd fall into bed unwashed and unbrushed, feeling alternately liberated and guilty. When we were little and

35

I did this, Mellie would complain to Mother, "She went to bed without washing *or* brushing."

Mother would say, "Don't tattle, Mellie. Janie, get up and brush your teeth."

I'd trot to the bathroom and move the brush over my teeth once and then get back into bed, sticking my tongue out at Mellie. We were past that kind of bickering now, and Mellie's presence in the room made me feel a little less upset. But then she asked, "Did you have a good time?"

"Great," I answered with too much enthusiasm. "Absolutely great."

"Janie, are you in some kind of trouble or something? I mean, do you want to talk about anything? You seem so strung up."

I hesitated, not knowing what I wanted to say. Mellie and I liked each other, we even cared about each other, but we weren't confidants. I mean she didn't tell me what her deepest feelings were and I didn't tell her mine. If I were drowning, she'd jump in to save me and I knew it, but I never told her when I was drowning *inside*. So her question surprised me. Finally, I answered her.

"Of course, I'm not in any trouble. Do you think I'm pregnant or something?"

Mellie looked disgusted. "I don't know why everyone these days thinks the only kind of trouble a girl can have is being pregnant. There *are* other problems."

"Well, everything is fine with me. Just fine."

Mellie got up from the bed. "I'm glad. I guess I'll go to bed now." But she hesitated and we just stood there looking at each other.

Then the strangest thing happened. I looked at Mellie and thought, *as long as I live she will be my sister*. I mean, if Tina and I had a terrible fight and stopped speaking we would no longer be friends. And husbands and wives can get divorced and they aren't husband and wife anymore. But even if Mellie and I never spoke to each other or if she moved to Siberia and we never saw each other, we would still be sisters, forever. The thought almost filled me with awe, and suddenly I started telling her all about the cowboy and my letter and my feelings about Peter.

When I stopped talking she thought for a while and said, "Have you told Mom and Dad about the cowboy?"

"No. I haven't. I took a post office box so I wouldn't have to."

"Oh," she said.

I looked at her suspiciously. "Are you going to tell them now?"

"Of course, I'm not! How could you think I'd do that? You don't trust me much."

"You used to tell Mother when I went to bed without brushing my teeth," I said childishly.

Mellie laughed. "I did, didn't I? Janie, that was a million years ago."

"Eight," I said petulantly.

Mellie put her arms around me. "I'm not

going to tell, but if your cowboy writes I think you should."

"You think I'm crazy, don't you?" I asked her softly.

She took her time answering. "No, I don't. I think I understand what you're feeling. I guess you're growing up and you have to make decisions on your own, but you also have to think about what you're doing and what you want. I'd like to help, but you know twenty is just as hard as sixteen, and I don't feel qualified. You probably don't believe that. . . . Am I letting you down?"

I slipped into my pajamas and sighed. "No, you're not. I guess no one can help much." I kissed her cheek and said, "Thanks anyway."

She closed the door behind her and I got into bed (it was one of those unwashed, unbrushed nights). I curled up, facing the wall my bed was against, and heard Mellie getting into her bed on the other side of the wall. I heard the click of her lamp going off. I lay there for a few minutes and then I reached up and gently rapped on the wall twice. In a moment, I heard her soft answering rap. I felt very close to her as I fell asleep.

CHAPTER VI_____

On Monday I raced to the post office right after school. I had been surprised to find out when I rented the box that it didn't have a key, but a combination lock that opened like a safe. My fingers felt icy as I followed the number code right and left. When the box sprung open, I peered inside and then stepped back. I had never seen so much emptiness, and I never remembered feeling such disappointment. I shut the box and slowly walked to where I had chained my bike. I had to talk to someone sympathetic, so I pedaled over to Kathy's house, hoping she'd be home.

As I rang her bell, I was saying, "Be here, Kath. Be here. . . ." And when she opened the door I sighed with relief. "Hi."

She smiled, "Hey, come on in. You look like you want to cry."

"I do."

She put her arm around me and we started up to her room. On the way, we passed her mother's study, and I saw Mrs. Fairchild collapsed over her typewriter, her head on her arms. Mrs. Fairchild is a writer, the only one I've ever known personally. She writes novels about teenagers. I like her, but I always feel she's observing me, ready to put me in a book about a disturbed girl. She raised her head as we went by.

"There are cookies in the kitchen. I'd like to think you'll want milk with them, but Cokes are in the fridge."

"Thanks, Mom," Kathy said. "I'll come down for them later."

Kathy's room is the neatest room I have ever seen. She has it fixed like a studio, a studio couch, a chest flush against the wall, an inch-thick slab of wood on filing cabinets for a desk. Kathy designs clothes and she's good. Her drawing board is near the window with a taboret filled with different-colored pencils and ink next to it. I'd rather wear something designed by Kathy Fairchild than anything by Anne Klein or Liz Claiborne or any name person.

I sat in an easy chair and said with exasperation, "Your room is so neat, it's disgusting. You certainly don't get neatness from your mother. Her study looks like it could make the *Guinness Book of World Records*."

"I know. I get it from my grandmother. She used to say, "Neat room . . . neat mind.""

"Do you believe that?" I asked.

"Of course not, but I'll try anything to feel neat inside. It helps me design better clothes."

Kathy curled up on her studio bed, facing me, and I watched her watching me. "I told Tina to tell you about my cowboy. Did she?"

"Yeah, she mentioned it. You're a strange one, Janie Downs."

I shrugged. "I thought you'd understand, because you're so creative and stuff."

"I do understand. I guess it's just that cowboys aren't my style. Now, anytime you see an ad from a trapeze artist, let me know." She came over to the chair and hugged me. "I'm not teasing, really, I just don't want you to get hurt or anything."

"How can a cowboy in Wyoming, who hasn't even written, hurt me?"

"You look hurt already."

I smiled and said, "I went to the box today and there wasn't an answer."

"Well, there's always tomorrow," Kathy said. "Come on, let's go get those cookies and Cokes. I always find stuffing my face makes me feel better."

But there wasn't a tomorrow, at least there was no letter. I did the same thing I had done the day before, raced to the post office and over to my box. This time my fingers were trembling so much I could barely get it open. But when the box did open, all that emptiness just stared at me again. The box seemed so *silent,* too. It reminded me of waiting for a phone call and staring at the telephone. At times like that nothing seems as quiet as the phone that isn't ringing.

And then it was Wednesday. I biked at my usual easy pace to the post office and kept my fingers steady as I turned the lock. And there it was . . . a long, white envelope, leaning against the side of the box. At first I thought, *I bet it isn't even from him.* And then, *Of course, it's from him. No one else knows about the box.* I grabbed the letter and just looked at it. Now my fingers, hands, and toes were all tingling. In the corner of the envelope in a bold handwriting in black ink it said, "Box 64J, Trentville, Wyoming."

Suddenly, I knew I couldn't open the letter in the middle of the Filby Post Office, with strangers all around me. I ran out, down the steps, and biked fiercely to Tina's house. When she opened the door, I waved the letter at her. "It's here. It's here. *From him.*"

Tina reached for the letter, but I stepped back. "No. I have to read it first, by myself. Then you can see it."

Tina nodded, pushed me into a chair in the living room, and I watched her walk toward the kitchen. I opened the envelope and read:

Dear Miss Janie,

I was very glad to get your letter. I got a couple of answers, but you sound so nice and friendly that I'm answering the same day. Just so you know I want to write to you.

I guess I don't know much about sophisticated hearts, and I'm pretty sure I don't have one. And I guess, too, I've never thought much about how I feel about life; I just live. I'm telling you all this because I don't want you to be disappointed in me. I'm just a plain, old cowboy who has lived his whole life in South Dakota and Wyoming. That's why I wanted to write to a girl who has been places I'll never get to.

You say you want to know all about me, but there isn't much to tell. I was born in South Dakota, in a town so small it isn't even on the map. I knew everyone in the place by their first name. My Pa owns a small grocery store there, and I mean small. It would fit in one corner of one of the fancy supermarkets I've seen pictures of. Well, when I got out of high school, Pa just thought I was going to come and work for him. But I tell you, when I thought of spending my life in that store I couldn't breathe. So I just took off. Hurt my Ma and Pa a lot, I know, but I would have died there. Does that make any sense to you?

I had been helping neighbor ranchers since I was a kid. So when I left home I just started cowboying for real, and I've been doing it ever since.

Now I want to know about you. I guess you go to college. What do you study? What do you do in New York? I'm pretty ignorant about all of that, and I sure want to know.

I'd appreciate you're answering as soon as you can. It would sure pick things up for me.

Yours truly,
Duke McCoy (that's my name)

When I had finished reading the letter, I sat still for a while. *Duke McCoy*, I thought, *what a wonderful name.*

"Tina," I called, "come back."

When she walked in the living room, I handed her the letter, which she read quickly. "Well, at least he can spell."

"What did you think he was going to do, make an X?"

She looked at the letter again and then laughed. "*Duke McCoy.* What a phoney name."

I took the letter out of her hand and really got angry. "Now you're just being nasty. What about John Wayne? *He* was called Duke, wasn't he?"

A gleam came into Tina's eyes. "Oh, yes, he was. And you know what his *real* name was?" She didn't wait for me to answer. "His name was *Marion*. Marion Morris," she finished triumphantly.

"I don't believe you," I yelled at her. "I

don't believe you for a second. Obviously, you are making that up. *Marion*. You're crazy."

"It's true, Janie. Really it is. I read it in an article about him."

I put the letter in my pocket and said a little more calmly, "Well, just because John Wayne's name was Marion, doesn't mean Duke's name isn't Duke."

Tina had calmed down, too. "That's true, but you have to admit it sounds like a made-up name. He could be the Marlboro Man, practically."

Tina took the letter back and looked at it appraisingly. "And what is our little college girl going to tell the Marlboro Man she is studying? Roundups I?"

"I'll work all that out. Please, don't spoil this for me. You almost sound jealous."

Tina sat on the floor next to the chair I was draped across and was thoughtful. "I guess I am, some. It's so easy for you to throw yourself into 'relationships.' I hate that word, but anyway, relationships with boys. How many boys have you secretly had a crush on, even during all these years with Peter?"

"Not too many, fifty or so."

"Exactly. Now, look at me. I've gone out with a lot of guys. I've liked some of them. I've never gone bananas over one. I always feel so calm about the whole thing."

I patted her head and said wisely, "That's because you're afraid. Ever since your dad left, you haven't wanted to trust a man. It's obvious."

45

She looked up at me and made a face. "Yes, Dr. Freud. Don't you think that's a very pat explanation?"

"Well, sometimes the truest explanations are the pattest. We all like to feel we're so special, but I think we're partly all walking clichés." I sat back, feeling very smug about what I felt was extreme astuteness.

Tina nodded. "You know, you say such smart things sometimes you freak me out. I mean you play it so sweet-sixteen and then you say something like that. But I never consciously said to myself, 'Okay, your father dumped the family, so be smart, don't *really* care about another man. Play it safe and you won't get hurt.' I mean it just works out that way. I haven't done it deliberately."

"I know you haven't done it deliberately, but you always seem to stop yourself when things look interesting. Like Will Orloff, for example."

Tina stood up and plopped down on the couch next to me. "Will Orloff?" Why, he wouldn't look at me. He's a sophomore in college. Big man on campus."

"Maybe," I said, "but he's looking at you plenty, every time he's home. And you're looking at him, too. Just as plenty. You'd make a lovely twosome. All you have to do is make him aware that you know he's alive. Chrissie Orloff is in our gym class. Get friendly with her and she'll have you over to the house when big brother is home."

Tina looked at me with disgust. "You are

46

really devious. Behind that sweet-sixteen exterior is a conniving brain."

I put my letter in my pocket and stood up. "I know, but a little planning never hurt anyone. Think about it."

Tina snorted. "Just what I need, to like a guy who probably has the Sweetheart of Sigma Chi falling all over him. Janie, you are really a dreamer."

I smiled and pinched her arm gently. "Yeah, isn't it great? Dream a little, Tina. It feels good. I have to go."

Tina stood up with me and laughed. "I wonder what you're going to be dreaming about? When's the last time you saw a cow? Now you'll be counting them in your sleep. I'll bet you're going to answer his letter as soon as you get home."

As I walked out the door I called over my shoulder, "Don't be ridiculous. I fully intend to wait until tonight."

CHAPTER VII_____

I didn't have to tell myself to dream a little. I dreamed all the way home from Tina's house, all the time I was starting dinner before Mother came home from the store, and part of the time we were eating. I kept thinking about Duke's letter. He *really* wanted me to write, as much as I had wanted him to.

"Janie. *Janie*," my mother repeated.

"Oh, I'm sorry, Mom. What?"

"I asked you three times if you wanted more pot roast."

I handed her my plate. "Sure. Yours is the best in the world." Not even Duke McCoy could make me ignore Mother's pot roast. It was cooked until it was deliciously tender, and the gravy was thick and brown with small bits of tomato and parsley in it. The potato pancakes she had made to go with it were crispy and light with a delicate flavor of onion. Even the peas were just the way I liked them, cooked just enough not to be raw but still crunchy. I thought about how Duke would probably love a meal like this. I wondered if cowboys still just ate beans and drank coffee.

"Janie!" My father's voice cut into the beans and coffee. "Peter is here."

I looked up from my plate and was startled to find that I was still in the dining room at 428 Elm Street. "Oh, hi, Peter. I didn't hear you come in."

My mother had a puzzled expression on her face. "You wouldn't have heard the Filby High School Marching Band come in."

I smiled brilliantly at Peter and changed the subject. "Sit down."

"I am sitting down, Janie."

I laughed slightly hysterically. "Of course you are. Anyone can see that."

Mother and I cleared the table and brought in the dessert, a big bowl of cut-up fresh fruit. And then it started. Mother said to Peter, "Like some dessert?"

And Peter said, "I just had dessert at home."

And Dad said, "Oh, just a small portion."

And Peter said, "Well, just a little."

I thought of Duke McCoy and all the mystery surrounding him. My head was filled with midnight-blue, starry skies, and campfires, and cowboy hats, and horses, and blazing sun, and a man I didn't *know*, who had dark, brooding eyes, and couldn't breathe in a small grocery store in South Dakota. A man who had called me *Miss* Janie. And it just came out. "Peter, why can't you just for once say no and mean it? Just for a change. Do we have to play this same boring game every night?"

The room was so quiet that it hurt my ears. My mother was motionless for a moment and then started to quickly fill dishes with fruit. My father stared at me with an expression I had never seen before . . . dislike. And Peter laughed, but I could see the hurt in his eyes. "You wouldn't want me to disappoint everyone, would you?"

"No, of course not," I mumbled, uncertain of how to handle the awful mess I had made.

Somehow, by everyone talking at once and laughing too much and eating too fast, we got through dessert. As soon as he had swallowed the last mouthful, Peter got up and said, "I'd better get home. I've got a lot of work to do."

I walked him to the door and put my hand on his arm. "I'm sorry, Peter. I don't know why I said that. I'm really sorry."

He looked at me for a moment and then kissed my cheek. "No sweat, Janie. Everyone gets moods. I'll see you tomorrow."

I wished he had told me to go soak my head, but Peter was always rational and kind. Duke would have gotten on his horse

50

and ridden away, right down Elm Street. I just knew it.

I didn't want to have to face my parents, so when I got back to the dining room I said, "Ma, I've got a lot of work tonight, too. Can you clean up without me?"

My mother knew. I knew she knew. But she let me go gracefully. "Sure. Double duty tomorrow night."

I went up to my room and closed the door. I sat on a chair and stared out of the window at a crescent moon and a sky full of stars. I knew I should have been thinking about Peter, but I guess I was just a rotten person, because I began to write a letter to Duke in my head. A knock on the door made me jump. "Come in," I said, fearing the worst. And I was right. My father sat down on the edge of my bed and without giving me a chance to be noble or pitiful or anything he started.

"You were thoughtless and cruel to Peter tonight. Nobody, man, woman, child, or animal likes to be put down in front of other people, and that's what you did to him."

"Dad," I interrupted, "please . . ."

"I'm going to finish, Janie. Peter is a fine, kind boy and didn't deserve what you did. I can't believe you are really upset over a stupid, harmless ritual. So if there is something else bothering you, tell Peter. Don't take it out on him in the indirect way you did tonight."

I looked at my father and turned back to

the window. "Sometimes a person doesn't know why she says things. Isn't that possible?"

"It's my guess you know very well what that scene in the dining room was about. And if you don't, I'd start trying to figure it out, if I were you."

I didn't look at my father, because I realized something awful was happening . . . he was treating me like a grown-up. His words, his tone. There was no room for me to be Daddy's little girl, and I thought that was a pretty heavy thing to throw at me when I was having enough trouble. I heard him open the door. "Good night," he said.

I turned to see his back disappearing through the door. "Good night," I called after him, but he kept walking down the stairs.

I shut my door and leaned against it, looking at the room, which was warm and glowing from the lamp at my desk. I felt the beginning of tears in my eyes and I bit my lower lip to keep from making any crying sounds, and then I just pushed the whole thing away from me. *It doesn't matter*, I thought. And I sat down to write Duke. I read his letter a few more times and then I wrote:

Dear Duke,
    I think that is such a wonderful name; it fits you just right I'm sure. I want to tell you that I couldn't possibly

be disappointed in you. I've never known anyone like you before. I mean a cowboy is hardly a "plain" anything. It is such an exciting, *different* thing to be.

I know, too, just what you meant when you wrote about feeling you couldn't breathe if you stayed in your father's store in South Dakota. I feel that way here sometimes. I think I won't be able to bear it if I have to do the same old things and see the same people, if something exciting doesn't happen. But then, of course *you* happened, and that makes everything different.

I stopped writing and faced the inevitable. He had asked me what I studied, what I did in New York. Could I tell him I was just a high school kid, studying geometry, and social studies, and Latin? Could I say that when I was in New York I only poked around Bloomingdale's or went to the Metropolitan Museum (because my parents wanted me to) and ate at McDonalds. That was as fascinating and sophisticated as a quilting party. I could see Duke reading that and galloping off to the nearest Trentville girl, who would seem like Jane Fonda in comparison to me. I took a deep breath, whispered to myself, *You're not a habitual liar. It's not like selling state secrets to a foreign power*, and went back to the letter.

I am studying to be a writer. There is so much about the world and myself I want to express that I have to put it all down. I am writing a book now and hope to have it finished by the end of the year. I certainly will add you to my list of characters, if you don't mind, because you will give the book a certain extra quality.

When I'm in New York, I do the usual things. You know, theater, French restaurants, discos. Just last week, I saw a wonderful play, *Romeo and Juliet*, in a new modern theater. It's called a theater-in-the-round. The stage is in the center of the theater, and everyone sits around it on all sides. Of course, the actors have to keep moving around so that everyone in the audience gets to see their faces. Juliet was absolutely beautiful in a long, flowing white dress. Did you read the play in school?

After the play, I had dinner in a little French restaurant near the theater. It was very beautiful, with red velvet chairs and gold walls, and every table had pink flowers on it. They have wonderful food and wine. I ate frog's legs, though I must admit I always feel sorry for the frogs when I do that.

I am still living at home, but just until I finish school and can get my own apartment in town. But I want you to tell me what *you* do. How does a cowboy spend his time? And where are you working?

I am glad you wrote. I feel you must be an extremely interesting person and I want to know everything about you.

Write soon. I look forward to it more than you know.

Yours truly,
Janie Downs

P.S. You don't have to call me *Miss* Janie.

I reread the letter and was somewhat astounded at how easily the stories about what I was studying and what I did in the city had developed. These weren't all total lies, actually. I did want to be a writer, and I had written lots of short stories and poetry, but I had never dreamed of writing a whole, entire book. Once I had gone to a theater in New York like the one I described to Duke, and I had eaten frog's legs in a little French restaurant, with my parents. The restaurant had been small and crowded, with just plain white walls and ugly brown tables and chairs. But I've always felt a French restaurant should look beautiful, like the one I had made up. But all these things had been treats, not things I did regularly. As for a disco, the closest I'd ever gotten to one was a pathetic little job in Eastport, a town near Filby, that was especially for teenagers.

I wondered if I could become one of those pathological liars I had read about in Me-

55

lanie's psychology book. Maybe I'd get so bad that I wouldn't be able to tell the truth. I thought about that for about five seconds and shrugged. I knew I was going to tell Duke whatever I thought would make me seem interesting and special, within limits, of course, and I'd worry about my psychological development some other time.

I carefully addressed an envelope and put the letter inside. As I soaked in a hot tub a little later, I wondered what Duke looked like. And I wondered if he dated. It was the first time I had thought about that. I realized that just because he was writing to me it didn't mean he didn't have any girlfriends. I felt a strange feeling in the pit of my stomach that I couldn't explain. Then I realized that that must be *jealousy*. I had never felt it before, because Peter had never looked at another girl. I had always felt sure of him, and now here I was feeling jealous about a man thousands of miles away, whom I had never seen, and had gotten one letter from. I remembered what Kathy had said: *"You're a strange one, Janie Downs."*

CHAPTER VIII_____

The next morning Peter was waiting in front of my house when I left for school. The air was cold and there was a biting wind, and Peter took the collar of the quilted jacket I was wearing and pulled it up around my ears. I was aware of the letter to Duke in my tote bag and felt a strong wave of guilt. To make up for my transgressions I gave Peter a dazzling smile and said warmly, "I'm glad to see you." I meant it, too; I was always glad to see Peter. He was, I thought with a sharp stab of realization, my oldest friend.

Peter draped his arm around my shoulders (as he *always* did) and asked, "How about a good long bike ride after school?"

I shook my head and said, "I have to buy some groceries at the market and I promised

Mother I'd clean my room today, too. If I don't she said I can't go into the city with Tina on Saturday." When I saw the look of disappointment on his face, I added quickly, "But I'll see you Saturday night, right?" I didn't want to hurt him. I really didn't. "I know you're going to your grandmother's for dinner tomorrow."

"Great," Peter smiled happily, looking reassured as if nothing had happened the night before. "We can go to that new movie house in Eastport."

He sure is easily satisfied, I thought angrily. And then I hated myself for putting down what other girls would give a new pair of French jeans for.

That afternoon Tina and I had gym and for a little while both Peter and Duke left my mind. I was in a special gym class this year which had turned out to be stranger than I had imagined.

Last September when Ms. Reilly, the gym supervisor, was giving us our routine examinations, she had looked at me skeptically. "Stand straight, Janie."

"I am standing straight."

"You are? Well then you're round-shouldered. Did you know it?"

I answered with a laugh, "Nobody has ever mentioned it before."

She turned me around and said firmly, "You definitely have a mild case of kyphosis. A year in special gym will fix that."

Now gym is one of those things, as far as

I'm concerned, that is death if you're not with your friends. I mean climbing ropes and straddling wooden horses is not my idea of fun and games. I'm not one of those people who doesn't like to exercise, but there's exercise and there's exercise. So picturing myself minus Tina and Kathy in a "special" gym class, whatever that meant, was horrifying.

"Please, Ms. Reilly, whatever this kyphosis is, I'm sure I don't have it. My mother has had me inoculated against everything, even diseases that haven't been discovered yet."

"Janie, kyphosis just means you're round-shouldered. No pleadings, no beggings, it's special gym for you."

I left the examination and rushed to the locker room where Tina was. "I have kyphosis," I shouted.

She backed away from me and said with mock terror, "Heavens; don't get it on me. Whatever it is."

"It means I'm round-shouldered and Reilly has put me in a special gym class. I'm going to be isolated from all of you," I wailed.

"You mean all that kyphosis is is round-shouldered?"

"Yes, but it's enough to separate me from you, and who knows what they'll do to me in special gym. Put me in traction or braces or on crutches."

Tina expelled her breath with a loud noise and shook her head. "How come nothing with you is ever minor. *Crutches!* Listen, I've got to go for *my* exam now. Come with me."

I walked her to the door of the exam room and then decided not to go in again. "She may do something awful to me." I watched Tina walk toward Ms. Reilly with her usual beautiful, perfect posture. As she got up to the teacher, she very slightly hunched her shoulders.

I couldn't believe what she was doing. Ms. Reilly took a look at her and then a second look. "Stand up, Tina," she ordered.

Tina looked at her. "But I *am* standing up, Ms. Reilly."

Ms. Reilly ran her hand up and down Tina's usually straight spine and said sarcastically, "Isn't it strange, we suddenly have an epidemic of kyphosis?"

Tina widened her eyes and said, "Is it fatal? What should I do?"

Ms. Reilly pushed her away, "Well, I guess a year in special gym won't hurt even you." She turned quickly and caught me in the doorway and said to the both of us, "Just don't think either one of you is fooling me!" Then she grinned. "You probably don't believe it, but I was a teenager once, too."

Special gym turned out to be gorgeous. We had this young, right-out-of-school teacher, Ms. Baker, who was into her own method of correcting posture afflictions. The fifteen of us in the class lay on soft, foam rubber mats and Ms. Baker told us what to *think*. We didn't have to move a muscle, just think.

When Tina and I were in the locker room, putting on our gym suits that Thursday afternoon, I poked her and nodded across to Chrissie Orloff. "Hi, Chrissie," I shouted loudly.

Chrissie waved and walked over to us. "Hi."

"Hey, you're wearing your hair differently," I said, patting Chrissie's head. "It looks great."

Chrissie beamed with pleasure. "Gee, thanks."

"How does your brother like it?" I asked, ignoring Tina's pinches on my upper arm and my own feeling of being a rat. Chrissie was a nice, serious girl and also a trusting one. She fell right into my trap.

"He hasn't seen it yet, but he'll be home this weekend and I'll let you know what he says."

"This weekend! Well, isn't that nice!" I turned to Tina. "Isn't that nice, Tina?"

Tina glared and pushed me aside. I took her arm and Chrissie's, holding on tightly to both of them. "Chrissie, grab a mat near us."

The three of us padded into the small gym room and joined the other kids who were already stretched out on the floor. Ms. Baker, in a soothing, almost hypnotic, voice, said, "Now, I want all of you to pretend you are pancake batter in a bowl. Now, the bowl is being tipped and you, the batter, are slowly, slowly, oozing out. You are spreading and spreading into a huge pan. Feel the movement of the batter, feel . . ."

While Ms. Baker was spreading her batter

61

around, I frantically began thinking about how I could get Tina and Will Orloff together. It wasn't going to be easy, because Tina, obviously, was going to be kicking and screaming all the way.

"Now feel the way the batter is sliding gracefully in all directions. Slowly spreading, oozing . . ."

I tried to ooze and think about Tina at the same time, which was no small trick. She could, I thought painfully, sprain her ankle in front of the Orloffs' house, and Will would have to carry the pale and delicate Tina in. But, of course, five-foot-eight Tina was hardly delicate, and she would hop all the way rather than let Will carry her. A hopping Tina didn't seem to inspire romance. Or she could wait until Will was leaving his house and then run into him on her bike. But that would hardly endear her to him. She could call him on the phone and just say, "Will, you really turn me on." *That* was so ludicrous that it was even beyond the realm of fantasy and I laughed out loud.

Ms. Baker shushed me and I gave up thinking for the moment as the class was being instructed to pretend we were an empty suit of clothes hanging over a chair.

At the end of the day, while Tina and I were walking home, she confronted me. "What was the bit with Chrissie about whether her brother likes her new haircut? You have never been concerned about Chrissie's hair before."

I stopped and looked at Tina with irritation. "You really can be infuriating. You know you like Will and you won't do anything to help the situation along."

"No, Janie. *You* know I like him. *I* didn't say it at all. Let's change the subject. Did you write to Duke last night?"

I softened as she zeroed in on my favorite subject, and I took the letter out of my tote bag and handed it to her. "I was going to drop it in a mailbox on our way home." It's funny, but I didn't feel embarrassed showing the letter to Tina, lies and all. We were such good friends that neither one of us was afraid to expose even the ridiculous sides of ourselves to each other. I knew she would huff and puff, but it was okay.

She stopped and read the letter and handed it back. "For a basically upright, honest person, you make a pretty good liar."

We had reached my house by then and we stopped and sat on the step going up to the doorway. "Is that how you really feel?" she asked. "Like you won't be able to bear it if something exciting doesn't happen?"

I stared straight down at the walk and moved a piece of stone around with my toe. "Yes, sometimes I do. As Duke said, like I can't breathe, my wanting something different is so strong."

"Does that include Peter?"

"Hmmm. When I'm with him, I feel like I'm with my brother almost, if I had a brother. I know him too well. Now when I think of Duke, I think of someone unknown and exciting, and someone who lifts me out of what is so everyday. Don't you ever feel like I do?"

Tina was thoughtful for a few moments. "Sure, I guess I do, but I don't think of a boy as necessarily being the answer. I think of going to college, of finding out what I want to do with my life." And then she looked away from me and I could hear a catch in her voice. "Of my father coming back."

"He isn't going to, Tina. You know that. You just hurt yourself by pretending."

"You're pretending with Duke."

"But that can't hurt me."

Tina looked directly into my eyes. "Can't it?"

I was surprised by her question and rather than even think about a truthful answer, I got up, brushed off my rear, and said, "Hey, I've got to go clean my room or I won't be able to go into the city Saturday."

Tina stood up, too. "Well, go clean. I'm really looking forward to our excursion. Don't forget under the bed, too. The last time I looked I found a playsuit you wore when you were three years old, romping in the sandbox."

The serious moment had passed, but somewhere down very deep I knew I would have to answer her question to myself, at some time.

CHAPTER IX_____

Going into New York, in spite of what I had allowed Duke to think, was something special to me. Even though Tina and I did it about once a month, we still approached it as an event to dress up for. On Saturday morning, I carefully put on a flaring brown skirt, my favorite coral turtleneck sweater, and a beige, double-breasted pea jacket. The coral sweater rose above the collar of my coat and I knew it made my eyes look darker and gave a pink tone to my cheeks. I looked good and I loved the feeling.

I walked the three blocks to Tina's house and felt a faint smell of spring in the still-cold April air. Tina was waiting for me in front of her house, looking . . . well, looking so Tina. She was wearing a slim, black skirt and a long-sleeved, white shirt, with a black and white polka dot scarf knotted around her throat. Over it she had the red cape she had worn as Little Red Riding Hood. Black stockings and flat, black shoes made her look like pictures I'd seen of chic, French schoolgirls.

We walked to the station at a good, brisk pace, talking about what we would do when we got to the city. After we'd bought our tickets, we went out onto the station platform to wait for the train that was always late. I looked up and down to see if there was anyone we knew and then grabbed Tina's arm. It was unbelievable, just too much good luck or coincidence or whatever. There, just twenty feet away from us, was Will Orloff.

"It's him," I hissed at Tina, trying to look casual.

"So?" she asked calmly, but I knew Tina too well. There was a look in those cool, green eyes that I wasn't familiar with.

I pulled her along with me and went up to Will. "Hi," I said cheerfully. "Going into the city, too?"

Will looked at me blankly for a moment, trying to place which of the high school kids I was, but he didn't look at Tina blankly. He *knew* who she was. "Oh, yeah. Just for the day."

Still holding Tina firmly, so she didn't take off, I said to Will, "Why not sit with us and we can catch up on . . . things." It was a particularly dumb thing to say, since Will and I had absolutely nothing to catch up on, but he was looking at Tina and paying no attention to me, except to mumble, "Sure."

We found seats together on the train, and Tina and I sat next to each other while Will turned the seat in front of us backwards, so that he was facing us. "What are you studying in school?" I asked him so that we didn't all sit without saying a word.

His eyes were still on Tina's face as he answered, "Chemical engineering."

Tina turned her head from the window she had been staring out of. "That's interesting. I'm sort of thinking of majoring in chemistry in college." Now she was looking directly at him.

The three of us talked distractedly since what was going on between Tina and Will had nothing to do with conversation. I had read about electricity between people, of chemical reactions, but I had never been part of it before, as an observer. But the train was crackling with the current connecting the two of them. Their eyes would meet and then they would look away, only to a moment later be looking at each other again, as if an invisible magnet was pulling at them. Sometimes their glance would hold for a few seconds and at those times I would almost not breathe. I could feel the tension between them, drawing them to each other. They never touched even little fingers, even accidentally, during the ride, but I knew they were completely aware of each other constantly. Will seemed to welcome and know what he was feeling, but Tina, I could see, was struggling with emotions that frightened her.

As we approached New York and the train sped into the dark tunnel under the East River, Will said, "I'm going to be working at the library this afternoon, doing a term paper, but how about the three of us going to a movie and having a hamburger later?" He was pretending to talk to both of us, but his eyes were on Tina, and I felt as included as a ten-year-old who goes to the movies with her older sister and her sister's boyfriend.

"Thanks, Will, but I have a date tonight. I'll have to get home." I waited for Tina to say something, silently willing her to accept Will's suggestion.

Finally she answered, "I'd like that, but I'll have to call and check with my mother."

"There are phones right in the station. You can call as soon as we get out," I told her, determined not to let her change her mind.

When we got into the upper level of the station, I led Tina to the phones and put the right amount of change in her hand. Will and I listened while she spoke to her mother.

"Mom, it's me . . . Tina. No, we're fine. Listen, we met Will Orloff on the train coming in and . . . yes you do . . . he's Chrissie Orloff's brother. . . . Well, he asked us to go to a movie with him tonight, but Janie has to get home. She has a date with Peter . . . but I have no plans for tonight and I'd like to

68

go with Will, if it's okay with you." Tina looked at us with embarrassment and then moved as far away as she could without pulling the receiver out of the phone. She lowered her voice and said with irritation, "He's *very* nice and *very* careful. *For heaven's sakes, Mother*. No, we won't be late." Then she smiled broadly. "See you later." She hung up and turned back to us, looking at Will. "It's okay."

He put his hand on her arm and they stood that way, staring at each other, unaware of all of Penn Station, and me. Then he moved back from her. "Great. How about meeting me at the top of the Forty-Second Street Library steps at five? Then we can pick a movie. If that's okay with you."

Tina didn't seem to be able to think about what was good for her, so I answered. "That will be perfect. We're going to the Museum of Modern Art this afternoon, so she'll be nearby." I felt like a mother making arrangements for a child who didn't speak English, but someone had to take over, since Tina wasn't about to.

I watched him walk away and liked what I was watching. He was the craggy type, with thick eyebrows over bright blue eyes. His hair was reddish-brown and wild and curly. He was over six feet tall, making Tina look small, and he walked with tremendous vigor and energy. Tina was watching him, looking scared and astonished.

I decided not to make a big fuss over Will,

but play it very cool with Tina, otherwise she'd think I was planning the bridal luncheon. "Nice guy," I said, and then, "Where do you want to go first?" Another girl would have wanted to discuss the shape of his ear lobes, or what he meant when he said, "How are you?" or how many seconds it was until five o'clock, but I knew Tina was definitely not one of those girls.

In answer to my question she replied, "Bloomingdale's, of course." And we ran for a bus going uptown.

Bloomingdale's is *the* fabulous store in New York. It is the kind of place that is showing now what will be trendy next year. It is every girl and woman's dream or nightmare, depending on how much stamina and money she has. When we got to Bloomie's, as everyone calls it, we were as always staggered at first by the colors, and people, and counters of gorgeous "stuff." The main floor was all black and silver and looked like it was meant to be the background for a TV musical production number.

We wandered through the aisles, spraying perfume on ourselves and smearing sample lipsticks on the backs of our hands. Tina stopped and draped a purple feather boa around her neck, narrowed her eyes, and looked as sexy as she could. I put a red sequined cap on and she shook her head admiringly. When we weren't putting on scarves and earrings and bracelets, we were gazing at the other customers, who were also gazing at other customers. It was part of the Bloomingdale's tradition. We rarely bought anything. We just systematically went through the store, poking and admiring. When we had exhausted ourselves, we stopped for a hamburger and a Coke.

"Janie, you have been writing strange notes in that little pad you're carrying all morning. Why, may I ask?"

"It's so the next time I write to Duke, I'll remember to tell him what everything looks like."

"I don't think the Marlboro Man is going to be interested in Bloomingdale's main floor, or even their second, third, or fourth floor."

"I guess you're right. It's just that I want him to think I'm what he expects me to be."

Tina took a bite of her hamburger. "You really think about him a lot, don't you?"

"All the time." I finished my Coke and took some money out of my bag. "Let's go. We have a duty stop at the museum."

It was part of my deal with my parents. I could come into the city and just wander, but I had to also do one "cultural" thing. They paid the entrance fee to the museum for Tina and me, but we had to go.

We dawdled all the way to the Museum of Modern Art, stopping along the way to look in windows, listen to a group of musicians on the street, and eat an ice cream cone. It was three o'clock before we got into the museum. We went through the galleries, hating some things, liking others, and ended up in the outside garden. There was a huge statue of a woman with large hips and breasts. I gazed at her for a while. "Looks like my grandmother."

Tina stepped back and looked, too. "You know, you're right."

We laughed and then I looked at my watch. "I've got to go if I'm going to make my train. You can stay here until it's time to meet Will."

Tina nodded. "I'm nervous. I mean he's a sophomore in college and I'm a junior in high school."

"Yeah, but he really likes you. So just relax."

CHAPTER X_____

That night as Peter and I were sitting in the movie theater in Eastport, I thought about Tina in a movie theater with Will. I knew *they* were aware of each other's breathing, and shoulders touching, and that if he took her hand her knees would feel a little weak and her heart would beat a little faster. Peter was holding my hand and it was nice and it was sweet, but I had no other reactions. I leaned my head on his shoulder and he rested his cheek on my hair for a moment.

I thought about how I'd feel if it was Duke, and my knees and heart reacted. But this was Peter, dear Peter, who had helped me learn how to swim. Peter who, when he was a kid, had climbed up a very tall tree and panicked, and I had climbed up and helped him down.

Peter, who had given me my first kiss and first Valentine. I thought, *There's nothing Peter could do that would surprise me, and there's nothing Duke could do that wouldn't surprise me.*

Later that night, when we were sitting on the couch in our den, he kissed me and I wanted to cry. I tried pretending he was Duke and felt so guilty that I pushed the thought away. Then, I thought of eight-year-old Peter up in a tree and I kissed him back softly, like a good friend. He moved away from me and looked at me appraisingly. "What are you thinking?"

"Of the time you got stuck in the tree." I felt that was better to mention than Duke.

"Isn't that a strange thought when I'm kissing you?"

I shrugged. "I don't know. Is it?"

"You're acting strangely a lot lately, Janie."

I tried to soothe him, because suddenly I realized how different life would be without Peter. How alone I'd be. "I'm really not, Pete. You're just being very sensitive. I'm the same, really."

"Well, maybe you're right. You had a big day in town, and you're probably tired. I'll go home, I think."

"Yes, I am tired. You're right."

I tossed around a lot that night, thinking about Peter, and wondering when I'd hear from Duke, and how Tina's date had turned out. I thought about the edge in Peter's voice

74

when he'd said I'd been acting strangely. I'd never heard that before and it frightened me. I had always had the security of Peter being there. I'd never had to worry about dates on weekends, or whether anyone would ask me to the big dance, or who I was going to a party with. I'd never been one of those girls who came to school dances and hugged the edges of the gym, trying to look at ease and happy but whose eyes kept darting around, and who smiled desperately when a boy went by. What would it be like not to have Peter? It scared me, more than I had ever thought it would, I guess because it had never occurred to me before. I wasn't ready for that, not in any way. But then I thought, *That's ridiculous. Peter would never break up with me. That just isn't Peter.* And I felt much better.

The next morning, as early as I thought was decent, I called Tina. "How did it go?"

"It was wonderful. He's . . . he's awfully nice and I didn't feel too young at all."

"What did you do?"

"Well, first we went to a Swedish movie and then to a little Japanese restaurant."

"That's about as ethnic as you can get."

Tina whispered into the phone. "We sat and talked and talked for hours. It was easy and comfortable."

I was really excited. "When are you going to see him again?"

Suddenly Tina's voice changed from happy and excited to tight and cold. "It doesn't matter. He went back to school and said he'd call.

But it doesn't matter if he doesn't. I really don't care." She was self-protective again and I didn't try to argue with her.

When I hung up, I walked to the window in the living room and looked out. "Will, call her, or write to her, or send smoke signals. But don't walk away."

I didn't realize I'd said it out loud, until I heard my mother say, "What's that all about?"

"Why didn't you ever tell me the whole boy-girl thing is hard?"

"I thought I had. Maybe you weren't listening. Wait till you get to man-woman. Talk about hard!"

But I didn't have to wait until I got to man-woman to know about *real hard*.

Early that week I received another letter from Duke. This time I waited until I got home and was alone in my room to open it. When I unfolded the letter a picture fell out, and as I bent down to pick it up I saw a pair of dark, unsmiling eyes staring at me from the photograph. It was a picture of him, in color. I was torn between minutely examining his picture and reading the letter, and decided to read first and then gaze.

Dear Janie,

I guess you've already found my picture. I just want you to know that the reason I'm sending it is because I want one of you and I didn't think it was fair to ask for yours without sending mine.

I never thought I'd know someone personally who is a writer. It must be a hard thing to be. You know, even though you are doing all those city things, like going to round theaters, and drinking wine, and eating frog's legs, and all that, you sound so nice and sweet. Like if we ever met it wouldn't be hard to talk to you at all. When I first put that ad in the magazine, I thought I'd never really find a city girl I'd feel comfortable writing to or that I'd have much to say to, but you're different. That's why I want a picture of you . . . I have to see what a girl as special as you looks like.

You asked me what a cowboy does. Well, I'm one of those drifting cowboys. I don't stay all that long in one job, but go from place to place. I can't seem to get myself to settle down. I always have this restless feeling that pushes me on. I've been at this ranch for a couple of months and I'm going to stay till around October. I guess you don't know much about Wyoming, but I'm near Jackson, and it sure is beautiful. We're in a green valley, between two mountain ranges, and it's really something to see.

Mostly, I take care of the cattle, feed them, make sure they're healthy, help birth the calves, brand them, all that kind of thing. Come July, I'll help round them up and then take them up the mountain to the summer pasture. I'll go

with a couple of other guys and we'll
stay up there until October. That's the
part I like the best, getting up into the
mountains and being almost by myself.
I guess you'd call me a loner type, though
I get kind of lonesome sometimes, too.
But since I've been writing to you and
thinking about you I don't mind it much.
You don't have to worry, even up in
those mountains I'll be able to write to
you.

I'll be looking forward to that picture,
and hearing more about what you're doing. I'll bet you're the prettiest little girl
in New York.

Yours truly,
Duke

P.S. Can't say I remember that Romeo
and Juliet.

I picked up Duke's picture again and looked
at it closely. He was more than I had even
dreamed he would be, much more. It wasn't
just that he was one of the most interesting
and entrancing looking men I'd ever seen, it
was the silent, brooding, *deep* look he had.
His eyes were dark, almost black, and since
he was looking directly into the camera, he
seemed to be staring right into *my* eyes.
There was a strange sadness about him, a
searching expression. His hair was black, too,
and very straight. It fell over his forehead,
reaching to equally dark eyebrows. Pushed

off the back of his head was a tan cowboy hat. His nose was straight and his mouth full and very appealing. His face was thin and on the side of his chin was a narrow, very faint scar. He really was something.

My parents were not coming home for dinner that night so I knew the house would be empty for the whole evening. Usually, I didn't like being alone for hours and I would have called Tina or Kathy or Peter to come over, but that day I was glad for the solitude. I needed time by myself to get used to Duke's picture and to digest the letter. Now, after weeks of wondering what he looked like, he was suddenly a *person* . . . a reality. He was a man with straight hair and a *scar*, not just a fantasy. I stretched out on my bed and looked at the picture for long minutes. I stared back into those dark, brooding eyes and then I closed mine and wondered what it would be like to kiss him.

I remembered the currents going back and forth between Tina and Will, and now I understood how strong they could be. I saw myself walking with Duke on a dark spring night in Wyoming. There was no moon, just blackness, and the air was barely stirring. Everything was quiet. I stopped and leaned against the fence that outlined the ranch and Duke stood in front of me. He put two fingers under my chin and lifted my face up to his . . . only two fingers were touching me, yet I felt as if my only connection with the world was through those two fingers. He bent his head and gently, softly, kissed me. I felt liquid, like the time the dentist had given me gas . . . there and not there . . . here and not here. Then he put his arms around me and pulled me close to him, forcefully. He kissed me again, only this time not so gently, and I put my arms around his neck and held on to him tightly because the whole ranch was turning and spinning and whirling.

The ringing of the phone made me leap up from my bed, and the sudden movement coupled with the feelings Duke's fantasy kiss had evoked in me made my head really spin. I tottered into my mother's room to answer the phone, feeling breathless.

"Hello."

"Hey, Janie, what are you doing?"

It was Peter, and the last person I wanted to talk to was dear Peter. "Oh . . . I'm studying."

"Want me to come over for a while?"

"Oh, Pete, I'd love it, but I really have to study or I'll never pass my English test." I knew he was waiting for me to suggest that we study together, but I couldn't. I couldn't.

"Okay." He hesitated and then said, "See you," and hung up.

For a change, I felt like a nasty person. I seemed to be feeling that way about Peter fairly constantly. I went back into my room and looked in the mirror. "You're a nasty person."

As I went down to the kitchen to see what Mother had left for dinner, I remembered the question I had asked Kathy: *How can a cowboy in Wyoming hurt me?* Well, I sure was letting him hurt Peter.

Mother had Scotch-taped a note on the refrigerator: *Your dinner is in red casserole.* My mother, if the opportunity ever arose, would probably let me go to Europe in a balloon, but she somehow always thought anyone in her house would either die of starvation or suffer severe symptoms of malnutrition if she went out and didn't leave food cooked, and explicit instructions, written in words of one syllable, as to where said food was.

I must admit when I took out the red casserole and opened it, I didn't mind. It was filled with rich, golden chicken soup in which were floating huge pieces of chicken, mixed vegetables, and broad noodles. I heated it, poured a glass of milk, and sat at the table in the kitchen, eating and rereading Duke's letter. A drifting cowboy, not just a plain ordinary cowboy, which would hardly be ordinary to me anyway, but a *drifting* one. Someone restless, like me, and yet so different. *I* could barely stand being alone in a telephone booth and here he was going up to the mountains for months, practically alone. He seemed so strong and mature to me. He was the kind who would protect his cattle from rustlers, and cow fungus, or whatever disease cows got, and his ranch from outlaws. He was every movie and TV cowboy I'd ever seen — all the gorgeous ones, anyway.

I spent the rest of the evening dreaming, and taking a bath, and doing my nails, and then realized I would have to have a picture of me taken immediately. Tina could do that. She was good at photography. I curled up in my easy chair and wondered what he would think when he got the photograph and then said out loud, "No! Oh, no!" I sat down at my dressing table and peered into the mirror closely. What I saw was a pretty, healthy, sixteen-year-old girl, with long, brown hair and fairly innocent, brown eyes. I looked about as sophisticated as . . .

"Oh, no," I repeated, and then turned to Jasmine who had been dozing on my bed until my shouts had made her ears stand up. "What am I going to do?" I asked her. "I can't send Duke a picture of *that*." I gestured toward the mirror on the dressing table, which had held my reflection a couple of minutes before.

Jasmine stared at me coolly. "Big help you are," I told her. Then I went back to the mirror. Not only did I look young, but I didn't have anything mature to wear. Every girl in Trentville had jeans and shirts. Then I thought of a blouse Melanie had and ran into her room. It was a soft, white cotton with a low, scooped neckline, and it could be pushed off the shoulders. I held it up to me and felt a little better. But Mellie and I had a strict rule that we always obeyed. We could borrow anything from each other if we asked *first*. No taking and then telling. I went into my parents' room and dialed Mellie's number. Melanie went to one of those far-out colleges where kids could have things in their rooms like pets and telephones. It was the kind of school that had courses like "The Search for Selfhood." I waited impatiently while her phone rang, and then heard her voice.

"Hello."

"Melanie, it's me."

"Are you all right? Is anything wrong?"

"No, everything is fine. I just want to know if I can borrow your white, off-the-shoulder blouse to have my picture taken in?"

"Yeah, sure. But Janie, that's a summer blouse and this is only the beginning of April."

I was silent and then she said suspiciously, "What are you taking the picture for?"

"It's for Duke," I answered in a very defensive tone.

"Who is Duke? Oh, wait, don't answer that, I know. The cowboy, no? He's been writing?"

"Mellie, he's wonderful and so handsome and he wants a picture. What's wrong with that?"

"I don't know. Have you told Mom and Dad about him?"

"Not yet, but I *will*. Really I will. Thanks

for the blouse. I love you madly. See you around." I hung up quickly before she could ask any more questions, and very carefully worked out just how I'd look for Duke's picture.

CHAPTER XI_____

Tina and Kathy were waiting for me in Tina's room the next afternoon, when I arrived for the big picture-taking event. Tina looked at me and rubbed her hand across her eyes. "I don't believe you. What have you done to yourself?"

I faced her squarely and spoke as quietly as I could, considering how angry I felt. In other words, I yelled. "Well, you don't think I'm going to send him a picture of Janie Downs, girl adolescent, do you?"

"You look like you're applying for a job as a go-go dancer." She pushed me in front of her mirror and ordered, "Look!"

I looked. I had on Mellie's blouse, pushed way off my shoulders, and a black velvet ribbon around my neck. I had taken my hair and rolled it on top of my head in curls, and then pinned them tightly in place. I had really done a job on my face, too, using the brightest lipstick I could find and all the eye makeup I owned . . . liner, shadow, mascara. The final touch was a pair of dangling earrings.

Tina shouted, "Do you think that looks *good*? He'll think you're a crazy woman."

"Well, you're so smart. Can you think of something better?" I shouted back.

Kathy, who had been silent up until now, walked over to us and said firmly in a low voice, "Why don't the both of you shut up?" She took me by the shoulders and pushed me toward Tina's bathroom. "Go in there and wash your face. All of it. And take off that blouse, too."

"Kathy, I don't want . . ."

"Go!" she ordered.

I came out of the bathroom with a shining, scrubbed, uninteresting face. Tina was leaning against a wall with her arms crossed over her chest, scowling. Kathy motioned to a chair. "Sit down."

I sat and felt her taking the five hundred or so bobby pins I had holding my curls in place out of my hair. "Great," I muttered. "Now I'm going to look just like I always do. Just what I wanted," I said bitterly.

"Relax," Kathy said. "Tina, give me your comb and brush." I felt Kathy's hands pulling my hair to the back of my head, twisting it, and pinning it in place. I also saw the scowl leave Tina's face and an appraising look take its place.

I started to get up to look in the mirror, but Kathy pushed me down. "Wait! Tina, give me your makeup. Janie, tilt your face up to me."

She did the whole bit on me: foundation, powder, blusher, eye makeup. "So, you're just doing what I did. Why did everyone have a fit, when *I* used all the gook?" I asked petulantly.

Neither one of them answered. "It's *my* face, you know. Why is everyone pretending I'm not here?"

Kathy clipped a pair of tiny pearl earrings on my ears and handed me a pale pink, silk shirt of Tina's. "Put it on and then look at yourself."

I stared in the mirror, transfixed. Kathy had pulled my hair to the back of my head in a soft French twist, leaving little tendrils escaping here and there. My eyes were delicately made up so that they looked wider and browner, and my mouth was full and pink, matching the blouse. I looked older, no doubt, but also soft and warm and nice; sophisticated, but likeable. I didn't even scare me.

Tina's mother worked around a lot with photography and she had set up a whole darkroom in the basement. The three of us trekked down there and Tina took a roll of pictures of me. Then she said, "Go home. I'll bring them over tonight after they're developed."

"I can wait here," I said eagerly.

"No. You make me nervous. I'll see you around eight . . . with the pictures.

Tina and I curled up on my bed and went through the pictures she'd taken. "I only made prints of the best ones," she said as she spread them out. "You look good. Kathy really made you look at least eighteen."

I gazed at the Janie in the photographs and could hardly believe that girl was me. "That's a Jane, not a Janie. She looks like she'd eat frogs legs for *breakfast*."

"Which one are you going to send the Wyoming Romeo?"

I picked one up and handed it to her. "This one. It makes me look wistful and worldly, as if I've experienced *everything*. If you know what I mean."

Tina looked at the picture I had handed her. "I know what you mean. In fact, I've been thinking, if you were dating Duke, considering his age and everything, he wouldn't kiss you good night and just let you go home and go sleepy-bye. Have you thought about *that?*"

I was somewhat staggered by what Tina had just said. "No, I haven't thought about it."

"Well, think."

"Tina, he's not here and I'm not dating him, so I don't have to think about anything." I took the picture back from her and looked at it again. "It's dreamy. Thanks, Tina. I really appreciate all your trouble, even if you shriek at me."

"I don't think I'm shrieking enough. I still feel this whole thing is going to end in disaster."

"You act as if I'm some kind of idiot." I was annoyed again and wanted her to know it. "I'm not irresponsible, you know."

Tina sighed and looked pained for a moment. "I know you're not an idiot. You're such a dreamer, though. And you rush into things so heedlessly sometimes. Anyway, no matter what, I'm on your side." Then she walked over to the window and stood looking out silently. She turned back to me with a small smile. "Will called last night. He's coming home the weekend after next and wants to see me . . . Friday and Saturday nights."

"Tina, that's great!" I was about to begin deciding what she should wear each night, when I saw the guarded look on her face.

"He asked me if there was anything in particular I'd like to do and I told him I wanted to double with you and Peter one night."

"What did he say to that?" I was afraid Will would think Peter and I were too much part of the kindergarten set for him.

"He said it was fine. Anything I wanted." She smiled a big grin. "I think that it will be fun . . . the four of us. Then she looked away and the smile left her face. "I'm scared, Janie. I've never liked a boy as much as I like Will. I feel so . . . vulnerable."

I reached out to her and took her hand for a moment. "Tina, everyone feels vulnerable when they like someone. Boys feel the same way. Peter has told me that. But you can't go all your life running away every time you like a boy. It's exhausting for all concerned. Me, included."

Tina smiled again. "You really are a good friend, Janie. Do you suppose we'll be friends all our lives? Even in Wyoming?"

"Of course. I'll find a cowboy for you and we'll all four ride off into the sunset together."

When Tina left, I sat down at my desk and started to write to Duke. First I propped our pictures up side by side and examined them closely. We really made an attractive couple. I looked sexy but ladylike, and Duke looked sexy and masculine, but thoughtful masculine, not the kind that made you think he'd expect a woman to be knitting lassos and cooking beans over a campfire all day. I remembered seeing an old movie on TV called *The Lady and the Cowboy,* and that was how he looked. I liked the image. I knew I was a dreamer and that a part of my life I lived in a funny half-world of illusions. But so far it hadn't caused me any grief, so what was the harm? I began writing:

Dear Duke,
    I received your letter with the photograph and I'm so glad you sent it. You are such an interesting-looking man,

and I can tell how sensitive you are just by your eyes.

As you can see, I am enclosing a picture of me. I really look *awful* in it, as it's almost a candid shot. I mean it was taken right after I had rushed home from school and hadn't had a chance to hardly comb my hair. A friend of mine who is a photographer — she does things for *Vogue* and *Glamour* and magazines like that — took it, and I hope you like it, simple as it is. I have to admit to you, though maybe I shouldn't, I'm not the prettiest girl in New York at all. The girls, I mean women, there are really *gorgeous*. Even the kids look like they might grow up to be Miss America, or better.

I've been wondering about a lot of things since I received your last letter. Like, do you have any girlfriends? That's a dumb question. Of course you must have girls you go out with. You're much too good-looking to just be sitting home studying brands or something all night. That brings me to the next thing I've been thinking about. Where do you live? I mean do you have your own apartment or house or what? And where do you eat? I hope I'm not being too curious. And if I've asked anything so personal that you don't want to answer, I'll understand. But you said you were a drifting cowboy and I couldn't help wondering why. I mean, why do you keep moving from place to place? It seems such a lonely way to live. I think I'd just die if I didn't have family and friends close to me. People I could depend on, people I knew loved me. You're much braver than I could ever be, I guess, because living that way would really frighten me.

Things have been somewhat quiet here the last week or so. I've gone dancing a couple of times, and shopping a lot. You know, if you live around New York you have to keep up with the latest styles or you're just considered out of things. Even though I think a person is very superficial if she spends *too* much time on her appearance, a girl, woman I mean, has to care somewhat about it. I guess men do, too. I've seen a lot of guys who can't pass a mirror without gazing in it.

Well, I have to study some now, much as I'd rather write to you. Do answer soon.

Yours truly,
Love,
Janie

I had thought for a while before I signed the letter, "Love, Janie," but Tina and Kathy and I had spent hours lately discussing women "taking their lives into their own hands," and especially not always sitting around waiting for the man to take the lead in romantic things, and I really agreed with that. So, I'd taken the plunge.

My father always said if you believed something strongly enough, and you were sure it was right and it wouldn't hurt anyone else, you should act on it. Otherwise it was not a part of your life, just a part of your head. My father was like that, direct and honest. My mother and I played little games with each other at times, even though we both knew we were doing it. But you couldn't do any game playing with Daddy. He always went right to the point. He didn't care if I got straight A's in school, or if I won the Miss Clean, Neat, and Sweet contest in school, but he expected me to be a trustworthy person. It made life very hard at times.

So, even though it scared me and made me feel as if I was wearing a scarlet letter *D* painted on my forehead, *D* for daring, I signed the letter "Love, Janie." After all, "Love" these days didn't mean what it did to Helen of Troy or, well . . . Juliet. I hardly let myself think about how Duke would react to this, though two scenes flashed through my mind: the first was of him fleeing in terror from what he thought was a love-crazed woman, and the other was of him arriving with wedding license in hand.

I reread the letter and added: P.S. What do you think of women's lib?

CHAPTER XII_____

"Peter, we're double-dating with Tina and Will Orloff a week from tomorrow." Peter and I were walking to school the next morning and I felt relaxed and happy. The softness of spring was in the April air, and the forsythia was blooming in almost every yard. The blossoms were startlingly yellow, unreal, like the color on a child's wax crayon.

"Since when are Tina and Will Orloff dating?" Peter asked.

"Just started."

Peter approved. "He seems like a nice guy. I don't really know him, since he was always a few years ahead of me in school."

I cleared my throat nervously. "I know, and I've been thinking, I don't want him to feel we're babies, so we have to be careful what we talk about. . . ." I really wasn't concerned about what *I* would talk about, but Peter was so involved with high school things that I was afraid he'd turn Will off.

Peter looked at me cautiously and took his arm off my shoulder. "What do you mean . . . careful?"

"Well, I don't think you should go on too much about the basketball team and . . . I mean Will is so far past that."

Peter's face tightened and his eyes were deep blue with anger. "Well, I can discuss the latest Cambodian crisis or crop rotation in lower Yugoslavia. Does that meet with your approval?"

By this time we were walking down the school corridor to my classroom, but it was all done unconsciously. He was furious but he mechanically moved along next to me.

I was angry, too. "You know that's not what I meant. It's just . . ."

"That I shouldn't embarrass you with the big college man. Right?"

I had never seen Peter so withdrawn or heard him talk to me in that hard, tight way. "I'm sorry," I whispered. "I didn't mean to . . ."

"You seem to be saying 'I'm sorry' to me a lot lately. I don't like it." He walked away down the hall, leaving me staring at his straight back.

"The plot thickens," a voice behind me

said. I turned to face Tina. She raised her eyebrows. "There's an old Hungarian saying that goes, 'You can't have your cake and eat it.'"

"Oh, shut up," I answered irritably.

"You're right. Come on into class." She lightly touched my shoulder and walked into the room.

I turned back to see Peter reach the end of the corridor, and then I saw *her*. Her name was Clare Gordon and she'd only been in town a few months. She was watching Peter walking down the hall, too, and there was a look of unmistakable admiration and interest on her face. Clare was one of those girls who wasn't gorgeous, but she was really foxy. She was small and always reminded me of a playful lion cub; everything about her was tawny and golden. She was wearing a skirt, a pale beige skirt, topped by the lightest yellow sweater I'd ever seen.

Her hair was dark blonde and hung in waves to her shoulders; her skin was honey-colored, and her eyes a light gray. I never knew what any writer meant by "sooty" eyelashes until I saw Clare Gordon, but hers were long and definitely sooty. She was softly rounded, sexy, and at the same time childlike. The terrible thing was that she was nice, too. I didn't know her very well, but I knew she'd never go after anyone's guy and she knew Peter was mine. But the way she gazed after him made me realize she certainly wished he wasn't.

A small chill went through me and then I said to myself, *You're crazy. Peter wouldn't look at another girl. He's Peter. Dependable.*

I walked down to Peter's classroom after my French class, wanting to try to smooth things out between us. He was standing in the hall, talking to Clare. She was leaning against the wall, holding her books clutched against her, looking up at him with a sweet smile. Her hair was falling over one eye and he reached over and pushed it back, just as if he were used to pushing girls' hair off their eyes every day. They both saw me at the same time, and Clare said, "Hi," naturally and simply. Then she added, "I have to hurry or I'll be late for biology. Bye." She *would* be going to biology.

"Bye." Peter smiled at her and we watched her walk away from us. Her hair moved gently against her shoulders and her hips had the slightest sway to them. If any girl knew how to move her hips with good taste, it was Clare Gordon. Peter looked back at me as I put my arm through his, ignoring what had happened an hour before. "I'd better walk you to your next class or you're liable to be hijacked by some gorgeous young thing."

He obviously had decided to ignore what I was ignoring, too, because he put his hand over mine. "What kind of ransom would you be willing to pay to get me back?"

"Oh, at least two hamburgers, a milkshake,

and possibly even an order of French fries
. . . anyway, definitely half an order."

And that was the way we played it . . .
light, easy, fun and games, not facing in any
way the fact that I was not the same Janie
I had been two months before.

The next letter from Duke came in the
middle of the week and it drew me even
closer to him than I had been.

Dear Janie,

You *have* to be the prettiest girl in
New York, and the sweetest, too. Your
picture is really something and I have
it standing up on my bureau so I can
look at it whenever I'm in my room. I
live in the bunkhouse at the ranch. It's
pretty good, as bunkhouses go. I've
lived in some that are pretty awful, but
this one is clean and newer than a lot
of them. I share a room with another
cowboy. He thinks you're real pretty,
too. He laughed when I put the ad in
that magazine; now he's laughing out
the other side of his mouth, wishes he
had a girl just like you. I eat at the
ranch with the other guys, except when
I'm up in the mountains and then I
cook my own grub. I'm good at it, too,
with the help of a lot of cans.

I date some, but nothing that comes
near you. I take a girl to the movies or
to a dance, but nothing serious. Like I

said, I'm a drifter and the girls know it, so they're not too partial to me, unless they just want a good time. But most of them want to get married and have places of their own, so I'm not much for them.

I thought a lot about what you asked ... why do I keep moving from ranch to ranch? I'm not sure why. It's just that after I've been in one place a few months I get this need to move on. It's something that keeps pushing at me. Yeah, I get lonely, but not so's I want to settle down in one place. Hell, I'm not brave at all, it's just that putting down roots frightens me more than moving on. My Ma says I just don't want to grow up. You know, I've never talked to anyone like this in my whole life, not in person, and now I'm doing it in writing. I never would have believed it.

Our lives sure are different. There you are partying and dressing up and studying and here I am looking forward most in all the world to getting up in the mountains with the cattle and little else, just me and them and a couple of other guys. How come we have so much to say to each other, when we don't do any of the same things? Do you know, even the weather is different where you are and where I am. I know it's spring in your part of the country. Here it's still cold and windy, even some snow.

We're busy watching the cattle real close because more calves are born in April and May than any other time of the year here in Jackson. So we're up off and on all night, checking the cows. Just like people, they birth more at night than during the day.

Well, I sure have rattled on. I'm probably scaring you off with ranch talk, but that's what cowboys talk about most, I guess. Write soon, Janie.

Love,
Duke

P.S. I don't have a real opinion about this women's lib business. Out here most of the women work right alongside the men anyway. I'd guess you'd call that equality or something. Did you know Wyoming was the first state to ever elect a woman governor, back in 1924? I guess that says something for the Wild West.

I sat very still after I read the letter. I almost felt like Duke was in my room. I had found out more about him in those last few minutes than I ever had about anyone in so short a time. He had a face, from the picture he had sent me, and he had a full personality, from the letter. He seemed so strange to me, unlike anyone I knew. The strangeness fascinated me, enchanted me, and honestly frightened me a little. We *were* so different, our lives were so different. I sat on the floor with

100

my head on the edge of my bed and I let new feelings engulf me . . . the strong physical pull, if only in fantasies, that I felt for Duke, that I had never felt for Peter. But more than that, the feeling that I was in a place I'd never been before, thinking about a man who was a grown-up, in spite of what his mother said. It surprised me that even cowboys' mothers thought they were kids. A man was not a boy. Duke was a man; Peter was a boy.

When I came in late Friday afternoon I heard my mother and Mellie in the kitchen. I also smelled onions that were gently browning in butter. Mellie was sitting on a chair at the kitchen table, and Mother was at the stove, watching the onions.

"Nobody tells me anything," I said to Mellie. "I didn't know you were coming home."

"I just decided this morning," she answered as I went over to drop a kiss on my mother's warm cheek. As I put my hand on Mother's shoulder, I felt the tension in all her muscles. I stared at the onions she was stirring, watching them turn delicately translucent as they browned. Mother looked at me, and I saw the tightness around her mouth. *Something was very wrong.*

"You didn't do a load of laundry this morning," she said in a low, cool voice.

It wasn't like Mother to get angry at something like that.

I turned and silently questioned Melanie.

Mellie raised her eyebrows toward the ceiling and closed her eyes. *"Who* is Duke McCoy?" Mother asked, pronouncing each syllable of each word clearly and slowly.

"You told her," I shouted at Melanie.

"I didn't."

"She didn't," Mother repeated. "I found the letters in your desk drawer."

"You *found* the letters? You mean you were poking around in my very own desk."

Mother stared at me angrily. "I went to your desk to look for an envelope. The letters from this Duke person were right on top. I didn't *poke* at all. If you are trying to keep this person a secret, you are not very bright about it. Letters in clear sight addressed to *my* daughter from a Duke McCoy in Wyoming would certainly attract my attention."

"You read them!"

"I did not. And you might as well realize I am probably the only mother on this continent who would *not* read them. I am either incurably stupid or unrealistically noble. Now, *who* is this Duke creature?"

I told her the whole story, while the three of us sat at the table. "He's a nice man, Mother. He really is," I finished.

"I'd like to read at least one of his letters, Janie."

I shook my head, no. "Don't you trust me? Do you think I can't tell the difference between a nice, intelligent man and a crud?"

Mother looked at Mellie for help. But she stood up and got some milk from the refrigerator. "Leave me out of this. I'm just an observer."

Mother stared at the both of us for a moment. "Why do all children think all parents are the enemy? I want to help you . . . to . . ."

I touched her hand gently. "I don't need help. I don't."

"I'll bet," she answered tartly. "I'll have to talk to your father about this. We'll see what he says."

She had barely finished the sentence when he came into the house. As he walked into the kitchen he was wiping sweat off his forehead. "The Spanish Inquisition missed out on a prime instrument of torture by not using the Long Island Railroad to break down their victims." He took ice out of the ice tray and dumped it into his glass. "I'm just going to finish looking at the brief I was reading on the train, with the help of one very cold martini. Then we can have a nice family evening." He peered at Mellie. "Where did *you* come from?"

"I think the stork brought me."

He left the kitchen, shaking his head. "Very funny."

When I heard him go into the den, I turned to Mother. "I thought you were going to tell him."

"Don't you think it would be nice to let the poor man to catch his breath before I tell him his youngest daughter is running around with a cowboy?"

"I'm not running around, Mother. I'm just writing to him."

She pushed her hair back from her forehead and her shoulders sagged wearily. "Well, one thing leads to another." She started out of the kitchen to the den and Mellie and I trailed after her silently. My father was already in his favorite chair, reading a very legal-looking paper. He never even glanced up as the three of us walked in like a small parade.

"Janie is writing to a cowboy in Wyoming named Duke McCoy."

He didn't raise his head from his papers. "That's nice." Then he looked up. "For a minute, I thought you said Janie was writing to a cowboy."

"That is what I said."

He looked at me and then pointed to a chair near him. *"Sit!"*

I sat. *"Explain,"* he said. "Now and quickly."

Once again I told the whole story about Duke and me. "How long have you known this?" he asked my mother.

"I'd say about sixty minutes, give or take a few."

My father was silent and motionless for a long, long moment. Then he looked directly at me. "I think your mother and I should see one of his letters."

Again I shook my head no. "You've taught me to be strong about the things I believe are right. Duke is a good, nice person. There has not been one word written by him or by me that isn't decent and okay. I don't think it would be right for me to show you his letters. He thinks he's writing to me, not a clan. You either trust me or you don't. I'm sixteen, not a child and I know the difference between right and wrong. *You* taught me. You and Mom."

My father closed his eyes and then opened them and turned to my mother. "Fran, you know I think there were times we should have kept our mouths shut."

Suddenly he stood up and came over to me. He looked down at me with his piercing blue eyes. "All right. You don't have to show us his letters. And I guess there is nothing wrong with writing to a lonesome young man in Wyoming, as long as your letters remain strictly friendly, nothing more. You're correct. At this point you either know the difference between right and wrong or you don't. So that takes care of this Duke . . . Is his name really *Duke*?"

"What's wrong with Duke?" I asked belligerently.

"Not a thing. Not a thing." He went over to my mother and took her hand. "Is this okay with you?"

She shrugged. "I guess so." But then she turned to me and asked, "What does Peter think of all this?"

I jumped up from the chair and paced around the room. "*Peter. Peter.* Why does everyone ask what *Peter* thinks? Peter doesn't know. Do I have to report to him every time I mail a letter?"

I started out of the room and Mother grabbed me by my hair, like I was some kind of Neanderthal child. "One more thing. From now on, Duke is to write to you at home. No more post office boxes, as if you were a secret agent or something."

"I paid ten dollars for that box," I wailed. "Three of them Tina's."

My father dropped his papers. "Okay, just a minute. Let's get this straight. Mellie knows about this, right? Tina knows, right? Who else has been part of this when your own parents couldn't be?"

"Just Kathy. They're my *friends*!"

"And your mother and I are . . . what?"

"You're parents. You can't help it. You're both very nice people, but you're *parents*. You're not Tina or Kathy or even Mellie."

"And never the twain shall meet. . . ." my father quoted sarcastically. "Okay. Fran, can we eat now? No Duke McCoy is going to get in the way of my dinner."

CHAPTER XIII_____

I was nervous and it surprised me. Tina and Will and Peter and I were at The Beachside, a place I'd always wanted to go to, and I was enjoying myself as much as if I were at the dentist.

The Beachside is a huge ballroom that has become a real "in" place. There are two orchestras, so the music is continual. One plays the old big-band music and the other, smaller group plays disco and rock and roll. But the specialty of the house is the old, slow, romantic music my grandmother grew up with. The room has a gigantic dance floor surrounded by tables lit with flickering candles inside glass hurricane lamps. Multicolored lights glide around the room, making everything seem magical. Because they play all kinds of music, they get people of all ages, and I like that.

I was trying so hard to be mature and interesting, so that Will would feel comfortable, that I was sitting up ramrod straight in my chair and talking in a high, tight voice that wasn't mine.

"Who are you voting for in the November election?" I asked Will as if it was the most important thing in my life.

Will turned away from gazing into Tina's eyes. "Election? Oh, it's hard to say. I haven't really decided yet."

Tina raised her eyebrows at me and looked as if I were someone she had just met for the first time, as I said, "Well, they are both good men and well-qualified for the job. Don't think? I mean they both . . . "

Will interrupted me as he turned to Peter who was staring down at his hands, looking very embarrassed. "Hey, I hear you're big man on the Filby basketball team. How's the team doing this year?"

Peter lifted his eyes to Will's face and saw what I saw . . . real interest, but he didn't answer for a minute. Will shook his head, remembering back a couple of years. "I played center my junior and senior years, but we sure had a lousy team then. From what I hear, you guys are really tearing up the courts. True?"

That was it. Peter and Will started on a running discussion of every boy who had played basketball for the last four years. They stopped only to dance with Tina and me and to apologize for talking so much basketball. Peter looked at me triumphantly every now and then, and Tina and Will looked at each other as if they had just discovered there was an opposite sex. I watched them as they danced, and tears came to my eyes. It was an old slow tune, and Will had her as close in his arms as he could. One of her hands was on the base of his neck and her cheek touched his. Every now and then she would close her eyes, then open them, move her cheek from his, and look up at him. They never spoke, not one word. I was unable to stop staring at them and the yearning to be with someone I felt like that about was so overwhelming that I hardly had room in my body to contain it. I thought of what it would be like to dance that way with Duke, and I wanted it so much that a small, almost crying sound came from me.

"Are you okay?" Peter asked.

I was wrenched back to the table by Peter's voice. "Oh, sure. I'm fine."

"Want to dance again?"

"Sure."

When Peter and I danced, I kept watching Tina and Will. *That's what it should be like*, I thought. *That's what I want.*

"He's a nice guy." Peter said. "She really goes for him. He for her, too."

I nodded my head, agreeing. "I'm glad for her. It's about time."

As Peter and I danced and talked occasionally, I was aware of how lightly he held me. Once, he would have brought me as close to him as Will had Tina, but not tonight. We kept a polite physical distance between us that was matched by the polite emotional distance.

When we were all at the table again, Will looked at this watch. "I don't want to stay here too late, if you don't mind. I'm going sailing at six tomorrow morning, and I want to spend some time alone with Tina before I go home tonight." He said it without any embarrassment, and Tina looked at him with admiration.

"Hey, do you sail?" Peter asked. "That's something I've always wanted to do and somehow never got around to it."

"Want to come along tomorrow?"

"Thanks, but not tomorrow. Some other time I'd like to a lot."

"The next time I come home, we'll go out together," Will said.

Will liked Peter. He really did, and I was ashamed that I was surprised. If anyone had been a bore and immature that night, it had been me, not Peter. I wondered how I could get things so mixed up sometimes.

After we dropped off Will and Tina, Peter drove me home. We didn't speak at all, and I was more aware of him silent than I was most of the times he was talking about the team or a class in school. Finally, I mentioned something that had been bothering me. "I didn't know you were interested in sailing."

Peter took his eyes off the road for a moment and turned toward me. "Do you think you know *everything* about me?"

I shrugged in confusion. "I guess I thought I did. We've known each other forever, so I ... well, you know."

We had reached my house and I waited for Peter to turn off the motor, but he didn't. "Don't you want to come in?"

Peter gripped the steering wheel and looked straight ahead. "I don't think so, Janie. Look, we have to talk."

"What about?" I tried to pretend I didn't know what he meant.

"Janie, don't. We have to talk about *us*. Let's take a walk on the beach tomorrow. I'll pick you up at ten and we'll drive out to the Point."

There was no use in pretending any longer. Peter was right, we did have to talk. "Okay. Let's do that."

Filby was just a few miles from the ocean, and at this time of the year the beach was practically empty. The air was still very cool, but the sun was bright and warm. A few people were stretched out on the sand fully clothed, but with their faces being slowly tanned. One or two optimistic boys were fishing, surf-casting along the shore. Peter and I took off our shoes and walked along the waterline. As the freezing water swept in

111

and circled around my ankles I caught my breath. I loved the beach at this deserted time, and I dug my feet into the muddy sand, feeling it seep between my toes.

Peter took my hand and led me back to the middle of the beach. I stretched out in the sand and closed my eyes, feeling the sun hot on my face and every cell in my body relaxing in its reassuring warmth. When I opened my eyes, Peter was leaning on an elbow, looking at me. "Is it another guy, Janie? I don't see how. You aren't dating anyone in Filby. Sometimes I think it's someone you see when you go into the city with Tina, but you never stay for an evening . . . long enough to date anyone. So what is it?"

For a moment I thought about telling Peter about Duke, but I couldn't. How could I tell him I was acting like such a rat toward him because of a man I'd never seen. It was too ridiculous. "It's just me, Peter. I just feel so restless and unsure and . . . oh, I don't know."

Tears were running down my face into my neck, my hair was getting wet, and some of the teardrops were dripping into my ears. Peter tried to brush the tears off my cheeks and shook his head. "I've tried to understand, not to get angry."

"I know," I gasped.

"We don't have fun together anymore and I think we should just stop seeing each other."

I wanted to beg him not to stop being my boyfriend, I was so afraid of the aloneness. But for once in my life I thought of someone before me. How could I ask him to accept the way I had been? And I knew I couldn't change as long as I was writing to Duke. "Can't we be friends?" I whispered.

"Janie, we'll *always* be friends, but we can't be a couple anymore. I can't."

I saw that he couldn't talk anymore. He stood up and helped me to my feet, keeping his arm around me as I stumbled along. We walked along the beach for a mile in silence and then went back to his car.

All the way home I sat next to him, crying as silently as I could. My hands were clenched tightly in my lap and I kept looking down at them, so that they wouldn't reach out and take hold of Peter's arm. When we reached my door, he kissed me softly on the cheek and murmured, "I'll see you around."

"You're probably going to rush right home and call Clare Gordon," I said between sobs. How could I be doing this? How could *I* be accusing *him*? I was really out of control.

"Yeah, I may take her out. What do you want me to do, sit home and wait for you to grow up?"

I cried louder, and Peter reached across me and opened the door. "Janie, darling, go inside. Go talk to your mother. I can't help you. *You* did this, not me."

I went into the house hardly seeing where

I was going. I heard everyone in the dining room, eating brunch. "Janie?" Mother called, but I didn't answer. I went up to my room and closed the door and lay down on my bed, staring up at the ceiling. As the tears trickled down my face I did something I had always done as a little girl. When a teardrop reached the corner of my mouth, I caught it with my tongue, feeling closer to myself as I tasted the saltiness.

When I heard the door open, I turned on my side away from whoever it was. "Janie? Janie, darling, what is it?" my mother asked softly. Her hand touched my shoulder and as I felt its light pressure I turned and threw myself into her arms, crying out loud. She held me close to her, rocking me in her arms. She kissed my cheek and kept brushing the hair off of my face. "It's all right. Everything is going to be all right."

As she held me, the tears slowed up and the cries quieted. "What happened?"

"Peter isn't going to see me anymore. Not as a boyfriend, anyway."

"Why?" she asked, astounded.

"I've been so awful to him, ever since I started writing to Duke and he's . . . he's had it." The crying started again and I sat up on the bed with my head on my knees.

"Is Duke worth it?" There was astonishment in Mother's voice as she reached over to the table next to my bed and pulled some Kleenex out of a box. She pushed my face up and mopped away the tears. Our eyes met and she questioned me again without repeating the words.

I leaned against my pillow and thought about Duke's letters, and the way they made me feel, and the way I had always felt about Peter. "Yes. I think so. I *want* to feel the way I do when I read a letter from Duke."

My mother looked worried, but she just got up and began hanging up some of the clothes I'd left thrown around the room. "I think you're crazy. I don't really understand you at all. Giving up seeing a boy like Peter for . . . for some mail. But you're the one dating Peter, not me."

She sat down on my bed and put her hand on my knee. "You know, some girls, some women, can care about two boys or men at the same time and be relaxed and happy and kind to them both . . . and some can't. You're obviously one who can't. I think you should remember that . . . always. I'm like that, too. Maybe I passed it on to you in some strange way."

She kissed the top of my head and went out of the room. I felt calmer. I *had* gotten myself into this situation; it hadn't been foisted on me. So now I had to figure out how to manage in it . . . and there was Duke, out there somewhere. I walked around my room restlessly, straightening things on my desk that didn't need straightening; combing my hair; even picking up a few socks from under the bed.

Then I sat down at the desk and started a

letter to Duke, because it was the only thing I could think of to do except cry.

Dear Duke,

I don't know why I'm telling you this, because it was really nothing *serious*, but there was this boy I had been seeing for a while and today I decided not to see him anymore. I mean he was just a *boy* compared to you and it just got to be boring. He just doesn't have the depth that you have. So now I'm going to devote myself to my studies and my writing and give up all the frivolous things in life. I thought you'd like to know. It will also give me more time to write to you. By the way, I think you should start writing to me at home; my address is on the envelope. It will be more convenient for me that way. My mother thinks so, too.

Write soon and tell me more and more about you and your life. It's like a TV show or a movie.

Yours truly,
Love,
Janie

P.S. Do you ever feel that things are just more than you can understand? I mean that life is so strange and sometimes so sad?

As I was addressing the envelope Mellie came into my room and sat down on the bed.

I wiped away the tears that were trickling down my face again and sniffed as quietly as I could. There's one thing I'll say about Mellie, she knows when not to call attention to the obvious. She ignored the tears and said softly, "Look, things may be a little tough for you on weekends for a while. I mean you're used to always having Peter around, so if you'd like to come up to school sometime, feel free. I can put you up in my room and we can just knock around for a couple of days."

I shook my head, sighed, and sat down next to her. "I haven't thought about weekends. But I guess they will be . . . different. Sure, I'd like to come up to see you. Thanks."

I put my letter to Duke in her hand and said, "Would you mail this for me on your way back to school? I'd like him to get it as soon as possible."

"Did you tell him about Peter?"

"Yes. I wanted to."

Mellie stared down at the envelope. "You sure are giving up a lot for . . . well, you're either very brave or very dumb. I don't know which."

"That makes two of us."

Before I went to bed that night I called Tina and told her everything that had happened. She just listened and didn't say much, which seemed strange for Tina, but I was glad I didn't have to cope with her giving me the wisdom of the ages. Before I hung up I asked, "You okay, Tina? Was your weekend okay with Will? I'm sorry. I'm so involved with *me* that I didn't think much about you."

"It was great. Fine."

She said it, but I didn't believe her.

CHAPTER XIV ————

When the alarm went off the next morning, I reached out from under the blankets and switched it off. As I snuggled deeper under the yellow comforter, I felt the familiar warmth of mornings in bed. Then, slowly, I was aware of a small lump of anxiety in my stomach. It spread over my stomach and up to my chest and neck, and when it reached my head I was totally conscious of *no Peter*.

Once when I was a little girl, I badly sprained my ankle ice skating. My father had carried me back to the car while I screamed. I remember him shouting at me, "Don't fight the pain. Just go with it."

I didn't know what he was talking about at the time, but now I knew, and I just let the awful feelings of fear and loneliness spread over me. And then I thought, *"This is ridiculous. Peter will be in front of the door when I leave, just like he always is. Peter is . . . constant and faithful."*

I wore my favorite slim jeans and a bright orange sweater. I even put on a little eye makeup and lipstick. I brushed my hair until it stood off my head in wild strands of electricity, and then stroked it down, until it was as shiny as a mirror. When I ran out the front door I looked up the block, knowing he would be walking toward me, but there was no one. I stood still for a moment, not being able to believe the emptiness of the street. I started to walk toward school, and I tried to concentrate on Duke. I had to have *something* to think about that made me feel good.

As I walked by Tina's house she was sitting on a step, waiting for me. She had never walked to school with me, because she always thought I'd want to be alone with Peter.

"I thought you might like some company," she said as she fell in step with me.

"You thought right."

We walked in silence for a block, and then I said, "I was so sure he'd be there . . . waiting for me."

"Who?" Tina asked, her green eyes looking at me suspiciously.

"What do you mean, who? Peter, of course."

Tina stopped walking. "Janie, when are you going to grow up? Why should Peter be there when you're mooning after some other guy?"

I pushed away the hair that was blowing over my face and kept walking. "Don't lecture me, Tina. I've got enough trouble. Peter's *always* there, so I just thought . . ."

Tina caught up with me and slung an arm around my shoulders. "I'm sorry. I don't mean to lecture. It's just you think of Peter as Old Faithful and he's a gorgeous, foxy guy. Take a good look sometime."

"Well, he's no Duke. You have to admit that."

"You're right. The closest Peter has ever been to a cow is a container of milk."

We had reached school, and as we went through the front door I saw Peter leaning against a wall, talking to a bunch of kids. I smiled at him with the broadest, most inviting smile I had in my repertoire of inviting smiles, one I used to practice in front of my mirror. Peter raised a hand in a slow greeting, but didn't move toward me. I stared at him, feeling embarrassed, and disappointed, and confused. Tina took my arm and pulled me with her. "Come on. You can't just stand there staring at him. Move!"

And that's the way the day went. I was spacy most of the time, and Tina more or less moved me from class to class when she was nearby. I felt numb, and like I was missing an arm or leg or something I'd always depended on. By the end of the day I was exhausted and just wanted to get home and reread Duke's letters.

When I left school, Tina was waiting for me, ready to walk home with me, and then I remembered how Tina had sounded on the phone the night before. Not only was I confused, immature, and spacy, but I was also a rotten friend. I was so involved with *me* that I had not even given Tina a thought.

When I reached her, I grabbed her arm. "You sounded funny last night. What's up? Something with Will? Tell!" The words tumbled out and I was out of breath when I stopped.

Tina smiled. "I'm awfully glad you asked. I mean, I like being here when you need me, but I like you're being here for me, too."

I nodded in agreement. "So, what's happening?

Tina stopped walking and sat down on the nearest lawn. I plopped down next to her and waited. Finally she answered me: "What I said last night was true. It *is* great with Will. I mean he's easy to talk to, he's fun to be with, he's interested in what *I* think and feel, and I'm, you know, attracted to him."

"Well," I said sarcastically, "no wonder you have a problem."

Tina shrugged and stretched out on her belly. "For me it's a problem. The more I like him, the more scared I get."

I stretched out next to Tina and looked right at her. "Does Will know this? That you're scared?"

"I told him a little . . . about my Dad and all that. And then he just held me close and said he understood and he'd never do anything to hurt me."

"So what more do you want?"

Tina sat up and hugged her knees to her chest. "My Dad didn't set out to hurt me either."

I felt like I was playing Simon Says, as I sat up, too. "Tina, what's done is done and what's gone is gone. Don't louse this up. Don't. He really seems to make you happy."

Tina smiled and pulled a leaf out of my hair. "He does, and I'll try not to make a mess of things. Really. It's hard, though."

Suddenly, we looked behind us and there was Ms. Foster, the crab who lived in the house that belonged to the lawn. "This is not a recreation area. In spite of what you two think."

I jumped up and pulled Tina off the lawn. "We were just going."

Ms. Foster raised her eyebrows. "Then let me see you go."

By Wednesday, every kid in school knew that Peter and I had split up, and I had to get used to people staring at me and becoming silent when I walked up to them. The girls were almost all sweet and tried to show me in some way that they sympathized. The ones I knew came up and said something or patted my shoulder when I walked by them. The ones I didn't know very well would smile across the room at me. It helped. The boys either ignored me, were embarrassed by my very presence, or moved in on me. I was fair game now that Peter was not around.

At the end of the day, Sally Feldstein, a girl I didn't know too well, who sat next to me in math, came over to me. "Hey, I'm having a party Saturday night. Want to come?"

"A party?" I asked, sounding as if she'd suggested running away from home with the local molester.

She smiled at my terror. "Lots of kids are coming alone. Or you could ask someone if you want." She hesitated and then said, "I've asked Peter and he may bring someone. He's not sure, but I don't think that should stop you."

"It's as good a reason as any to stop me."

Sally put her hand on my arm. "Listen, Janie, when I broke up with Fred I locked myself in the house for a month. It was a mistake. You've got to be part of the human race. Come to the party!"

Before I could change my mind, I said, "Okay." As she walked away I yelled after her, "Hey, thanks."

She turned back to me and waved. "You do the same thing for someone sometime. It's the best kind of togetherness."

That night while we were having dinner the phone rang. My father got up and went into the kitchen to answer. "I'm expecting a call from a client." A moment later he was back in the dining room. "It's for you. A boy. Not Peter."

"A *boy*?"

My father sat down and picked up his coffee cup. "Yes. *Boy*. You know, the opposite of girl."

My hand was sweating as I picked up the receiver. "Hello."

"Janie? This is Jack Zoner. How'd you like to go to Sally's party with me? We'd make a beautiful couple."

Jack Zoner is not *exactly* what you'd call a creep. He's good-looking and smart, but he's creepy. He's conceited and he's one of those boys who is always touching you. Not that he does anything you could call fresh, but he's always holding your hand, or putting his arm around you, or patting your cheek. He's always so much *there*. But at the moment anything seemed better than walking into Sally's alone.

"Sure, Jack. I'll go with you. What time?"

"I'll pick you up at eight. Look gorgeous!"

I closed my eyes as I hung up and wished Jack Zoner had picked on someone else, or that he'd fall madly in love with someone by Saturday and break the date.

As I lay in bed that night, I felt tears rolling down my face. "Oh, Duke," I said aloud. "Why can't you be nearer?"

I got up, turned on the lamp next to my bed, and took the picture of him I kept in my mirror. I stared at it and touched his cheek. The dark eyes looked back at me and I felt a wonderful warmth seep through me. I looked at the full mouth and almost felt it gently kissing me. His hands were on each side of my head and he pressed my face against his shoulder. "You're worth all of this," I whispered. "I know it."

That weekend was the first one I spent without Peter. I was determined to make it bearable. After all, I had made the situation I was in myself. I wanted to have what Duke gave me, so I had to act like a grown-up.

On Saturday, I cleaned my room until it didn't look like mine at all. My mother examined it with interest. "Do you think you can break up with a boy regularly? It makes you act like a housewife in a TV commercial for detergent."

I decided I was going to look ravishing at Sally's party. I washed my hair twice, set it in three different ways, and then let it hang down my back after all. I tried on every combination of skirts, jeans, blouses, and sweaters I owned, making the room look like mine again as I dropped things on the floor and threw them across the bed.

As I was examining myself in the mirror, wearing sneakers, underpants, a silver blouse, and a beach hat I'd found on the shelf, Tina came in. "It's *you*," she said. "All you need is a basket of flowers."

"Well, I'm trying to look different."

"You sure do. Zoner will regret the day he

ever dialed your number. Serves him right. Old Mr. Handy."

Tina pushed some clothes to the side and sat down on my bed. I took a good look at her and saw that her usually pale cheeks were flushed and her green eyes had an expression in them very unlike Tina ... almost coy.

"You look like you have a secret that makes you feel very superior."

"Will called this morning. He's coming down next weekend ... just to see me. So I won't think he's disappeared, he said."

"Oh, Tina," I said softly. "See. He's a good guy."

I must have looked wistful, because she touched my arm and said, "If you can dig up someone other than Zoner, maybe we could all ... "

"It's okay, Tina. I can take care of myself."

Tina hesitated a moment and then said very quickly, "You know, if you've changed your mind ... all you'd have to do is call Peter, and ... "

"No!" I shouted.

"Okay. Okay."

Tina went downstairs, and I started trying on clothes again. But my enthusiasm had waned. The idea of going to a party with Jack was becoming less and less attractive. I thought of how secure I'd always felt going out with Peter. *All you'd have to do is call. . . .*

I looked up and Tina was standing there

with a flat envelope in her hand. "It's for you . . . from him."

"It's such a funny shape for a letter . . . much bigger. I wonder what it is." I kept turning it over, pressing it.

"Well, for heaven's sake, open it," Tina said.

I ripped open the envelope and it was a picture and a letter. The picture was much bigger than a normal snapshot. It was of Duke, sitting on a beautiful, sleek horse. His hat was on the back of his head, like the first picture, but this time he was smiling at me.

Tina looked over my shoulder. "Hi ho, Silver."

I pushed her away with annoyance. "You have to admit, he looks wonderful. Like nothing you've seen in Filby."

"I have to admit it," she said softly, and left.

I opened the letter and read it stretched out on my bed.

Dear Janie,

I received your letter and even though I have no right to say this, I was glad that you stopped seeing that boy . . . whoever he was.

I used to think a lot about your going out with other guys, and I wanted to sock them. I shouldn't tell you this, but I've been thinking of you as *my girl*. Even though we're so far apart, I *feel* like you're my girl. I guess I've fallen a little in love with you. How could I not? How could any guy not? You're so pretty and sweet and smart. I don't mean that you shouldn't date other guys. I couldn't ask you that. But I'm glad there is no one you're real interested in. The same goes for me.

The picture is because I wanted you to get to know my horse a little. His name is Oscar, after a guy I once knew who taught me how to rope and ride and just about everything else. I wanted you to know I can smile, too. In the last picture I sent you I was so serious, but thinking of you makes me smile.

It's still real cold here, but we know spring isn't too far away. I got to go now. Some of the guys are waiting for me to go into town with them. But I wanted to mail this to you right off.

Good-bye, sweet Janie.

Love,
Duke

I didn't move after I read the letter. I just hung on to it. It was as if all my dreams had come true. This strange, mature man who smiled at me from a horse, loved me. Me, Janie. He thought of me as his girl. I'd never been more than one hundred miles from Filby and I was the girl of a cowboy in Wyoming.

Nothing scared me now . . . not going to

Sally's party, not Jack Zoner, not Peter. I was Janie Downs . . . pretty, smart, healthy, and I was Duke McCoy's girl. Who else in Filby, New York, could say that?

I looked great at Sally's party. I knew it. I had put on more eye makeup than usual, which made my eyes look bigger and deeper. I'd borrowed my mother's reddest lipstick and felt like someone out of a forties movie. I finally decided to wear a brown skirt, not jeans, and a high-necked pink sweater. I put on my one pair of heels and brown mesh pantyhouse.

Even Zoner stopped looking in every mirror he passed and said, "You look pretty good, kid."

I pushed his arm off my shoulders as he said it. "You've made my night," I answered, and the creep believed me.

I saw Peter as soon as we got to Sally's. He looked . . . well, like Peter . . . handsome. He saw me, too, as soon as I came in. I smiled at him, and then I saw Clare. She was all golden, as usual. Tight beige pants, a beige sweater. She had pulled her dark blonde hair up to the top of her head, and it hung in waves from a yellow flower. She smiled at me hesitantly and looked away. Peter waved his hand but didn't come over. When he saw Jack Zoner, a quick look of disbelief and puzzlement slipped over his face and then disappeared.

I was aware of Peter all night. While I was

listening to someone talking, while I was eating, or dancing, I knew exactly where he was every minute. Every now and then I'd look at him and smile dazzlingly. I felt an emptiness deep in me, watching him ignore me. But I'd repeat to myself, *Duke McCoy loves me.*

When I danced with Jack, I tried to pretend he was Duke. But even Duke wasn't able to make me unaware of Jack. I had closed my eyes, thinking that would help, when I felt a different pair of arms around me, Peter.

My stomach lurched in a strange way and I smiled at him. "I'm glad you came over."

"Janie. Why a guy like Zoner? He's the pits."

I shrugged. "I know, but I didn't want to come alone. And he asked me. *You* didn't come alone, I notice. Why should I?"

Peter shook his head. "You're right. I'll keep out of your life." But his arms tightened around me.

I felt what I had always felt in Peter's arms . . . safe. But my mind was filled with the picture of a man sitting on a horse, smiling.

CHAPTER XV_____

Sunday brunch in my house is a must. That is, everyone who is at home has to appear. When Mellie and I first started dating, we'd sleep late, and since my parents often went out to dinner on Saturday night, sometimes the whole weekend would go by without the family sitting down together for a meal until Sunday night. My father finally made the rule: Everyone out of bed and ready to eat by eleven-thirty on Sunday mornings ... no matter what. It was also the meal where everyone cooked something, except Dad.

My father did a lot around the house. He'd do the laundry, run the vacuum, clean the bathroom, but he'd never cook. He hated it, and just wouldn't even try. So this morning, Mother had made light, fluffy waffles with hot maple syrup and golden butter, and I had fried the bacon just right and made blueberry muffins. Dad did watch the coffee that was perking in the electric coffee maker. He seemed to feel that was a valid contribution, though Mother and I did not.

I was feeling very good. I had survived my first Saturday night without Peter; my first party without Peter as a date; and I had survived Jack Zoner, too. I had even dreamed about Duke the night before. The dream had become unfocused, but fragments of it reached my consciousness now and then. I remembered Duke holding my hand, and walking along Elm Street with me. He stopped and reached for my other hand and swung them both back and forth while I laughed.

I was caught up in the dream-picture when I heard my father say, "I went into your room last night when it started to rain, and shut the window."

I waited for him to go on, knowing *that* couldn't be what he was telling me.

"I saw the picture of that Duke fellow . . . on a horse."

I watched him carefully. "That's what he rides . . . a horse."

My father cleared his throat. "I also noticed that you had put away Peter's picture. Right?"

"I don't like your poking around my room," I said firmly.

"Janie, it is very difficult to go into a room and shut a window with one's eyes closed."

"Okay. Yes. I put away Peter's picture. I also put away my Teddy bear a few years ago. You never commented on *that*."

We all ate in silence for a few minutes. The waffles, which had melted around my tongue a little before, now stuck in my throat.

Then my father reached over and touched my hand. "I'm driving over to Easthampton after brunch to bring some papers to a client who is sick. Want to come along?"

I nodded and smiled tentatively, glad we had gotten past the bad moments.

The first ten minutes we were riding neither one of us said a word. I looked at my father sideways and noticed with a fleeting stab in my stomach that he had more gray in his hair and less hair altogether. The firm line of his chin had softened and there were lines around his eyes. He was older, and it hurt. I waited for him to say *something*.

But I was the one who spoke first. "You don't love me anymore!"

Dad looked at me with a startled expression. "Janie, no!"

We were approaching an exit from the highway we were on and my father turned into it. We drove a few blocks and he parked on a deserted street.

"Janie, I'll *always* love you. You're my ...

little girl, even though you're growing up. And that's it."

"That's what?" I asked.

"I used to know you. I used to understand you. Now I don't. I mean this whole business with Peter and this . . . Duke person. I don't understand it."

I looked out the window. "I can't explain, because I don't know if *I* understand it. I'm confused and I feel all alone a lot of the time."

Dad put his arm around me and I put my head on his shoulder. "I know. I know it's tough being your age. I remember that . . . sometimes. But it's tough being a parent, too."

I raised my head and looked at him. "Really?"

"Really!"

I sighed loudly. "That's not much help to me."

Dad took his arm away. "You're not someplace I can help much. But Janie, I do love you. . . ."

We were suddenly both embarrassed by our spontaneous confessions and Dad started the car quickly. We dropped off the papers and started the two-hour drive home, but as we passed the tiny amusement park where we used to go when I was a little girl, my father swung into its parking lot. He grabbed my hand and pulled me out of the car. "Come on," he said.

I followed him, feeling ridiculous and

joyous. We jumped on the merry-go-round and as it went around and around and the horses went up and down, I laughed out loud. My horse was white and his mane was flying back the way my hair was. The wind rushed against my face and the music filled my head. The merry-go-round whirled around and I had never felt as happy and free as I did that moment. My father, who was on the horse next to mine, yelled over the wind, "Go for the brass ring."

I leaned out and reached wildly, missing each time and not caring. I leaned back on the horse, laughing louder. I was happy, and it had nothing to do with Peter or Duke or my father. It was just because I was Janie Downs on a merry-go-round.

When we got off, we went to the ice cream booth and bought triple-scoop cones and wandered around the park eating them and catching the ice cream as it dribbled down our fingers and chins. When we finally went back to the car, Dad kissed me on the cheek and said, "That was for old times' sake. But I guess we won't be going back there again. Maybe when you have children. Someday."

A lot of the time I don't really understand my father, but that day I did.

Before I went to sleep that night, I wrote Duke. I was very tired, so tired that I could hardly keep my eyes open as I wrote the letter. With great effort I moved the pen over my stationary, yawning as I wrote.

Dear Duke,

I'm awfully tired because I spent the day with my father, visiting a client who lives hours away. But I just wanted to tell you I got your picture and I love Oscar.

I think I love you, too.

Yours truly,
Love,
Janie

School that Monday was easier than the week before. The kids were getting used to the breakup of Peter and me and were onto another couple who had run off and gotten married. It still took my breath away when I saw Peter and he would just wave or smile, but it didn't surprise me as much. I even turned down Jack Zoner when he asked me out for the next Saturday. I mean, some lessons you learn or else.

Kathy and Tina and I ate lunch together and I proudly told them, "I'm the epitome of the independent woman. Gloria Steinem would love me. I turned down a date with Jack Zoner."

Kathy drank some milk and wiped her mouth. "That's not independent, that's just plain self-protective."

"Or just using the old brain box," Tina added.

That was the way the day went, just an ordinary day. But that afternoon changed my life. When I got home, Jasmine was waiting at the door for me, meowing for a treat. I rubbed my ankle against her and reached into the mailbox at the same time, juggling my books and holding the door open. I took the mail inside and sat down on the bottom step of the staircase to go through it. There was another letter from Duke. He couldn't have even gotten mine yet, so I was extra pleased.

Dear Janie,
I can't believe it! You won't either! But I'm going to be in New York City next Sunday. There's this Wyoming rodeo that's going to play at Madison Square Garden. Well, they need one more cowboy, and when I heard about it I knew it had to be me. I just had to get to see you. We're coming by bus, and arriving at something called the Port Authority Bus Terminal at 12 noon on Sunday. Be there to meet me, Janie, dear. I can't wait to see you. I'll be in New York one week, with performances every day, but we'll still have time to be together.
See you Sunday.
Love,
Duke

I raced into the kitchen, threw Jasmine a potato chip (she loved them), and ran all the way to Tina's. I banged on her door, rang the bell, and yelled, "Tina," all at the same time.

She opened the door, looking confused. "What's happening?"

I pushed her aside and went in. "He's coming. Duke's coming to New York on Sunday. I'm going to really see him."

Tina took the letter I was waving out of my hand and read it. "*Wow*. Double wow! This makes things very different."

I grabbed back the letter. "This makes things wonderful. Exciting. Thrilling."

Tina and I went into the kitchen while she opened the refrigerator and took out fruit and cheese. "You're not really going to go meet him at Port Authority all by yourself."

"Well, of course I am. What's this all by myself bit? It's only a few blocks up from the station. I'll hardly get lost."

Tina sliced a piece of cheese and handed it to me. "What do you think your parents are going to say?"

I sat at the kitchen table and nibbled on the cheese. "I haven't thought about that yet." I paused a moment and then said, "Well, I just thought about it. I won't tell them right away, not until he gets here. Once I've seen him, then I'll tell them."

Tina poured some milk and gave me some. "Well, I'm going with you then."

I slammed my milk down on the table and said tightly, "You *aren't*. How do you think that would look, bringing my friend to meet my ... whatever he is?"

Tina busied herself putting cheese on a cracker and said firmly, "Well, if you won't let me come, then I'm going to tell your parents."

I was astounded. "You're a fink, a real fink. I thought you were my best friend, and you're a traitor."

Tina looked pained, but she didn't budge. "Janie, be sensible, I'm not going to let you go into New York, to that zoo of a bus station, and meet a cowboy you've never seen all by yourself. *I'm not.* So decide who you want along with you, me or your father."

I said triumphantly, "You can't go. Will is coming in next weekend. You're certainly not going to give up seeing Will to drag into New York with me."

Tina popped a cracker into her mouth and between chews said, "Will can come along."

I was astounded. "You're crazy, really crazy. Why don't you ask your mother, too, and maybe Kathy and Tommy would like to come, and Mellie could come down from school. We could pack a picnic lunch."

Tina looked a little rueful. "Okay, so it will just be me. It won't take all day, and Will won't mind. I mean it, Janie. Me or your father."

I knew I had lost. "You." I said. Though I never would have admitted it, I was glad she was coming with me. I was scared. It was one thing to be writing letters to an older man who was thousands of miles away. It was another to be meeting him in a bus station.

The rest of the week was almost psychedelic. I was dimly aware of the things going

on around me, but dimly. I didn't hear
teachers asking me questions in school, or my
parents talking to me at home. I left the house
twice without taking my keys and all in all
I was a basket case.

By Saturday I had lost three pounds, bitten
my nails off, and had cleaned my room four
times. That's how rattled I was. Saturday
morning, I was in my room just lying on the
bed when I heard a car horn honking loudly
in front of the house. I got up and stuck my
head out of the window. Will and Tina were
in Will's beat-up convertible. The top was
down and Tina looked up at me and waved.
"Come on. We're going out to the Point for a
hamburger. Come along."

"You don't need me. Didn't you ever hear
the old Icelandic proverb: 'Two's company,
three's a drag.'"

Will waved at me, too. "Come on. We want
a drag with us."

I figured I wasn't going to do anything
constructive at home and if I cleaned my
room once more my mother would take me to
the doctor, so I went with them.

On the way, Tina said, "By the way, I told
Will about the Lone Ranger. I had to explain
where we were going tomorrow. Hope it's
okay with you."

"Why not?" I answered. I leaned over Tina,
who was sitting between Will and me and
said to him, "*You* probably think I'm crazy,
too."

Will didn't take his eyes off the road, but

141

he shook his head. "No, I don't think you're crazy. I think you're trying your wings out a little."

I didn't like that. "Isn't that a condescending thing to say?"

Will shook his head again. "It's true, isn't it? Everybody does it."

Suddenly, I liked him a lot, because it *was* true. I had felt much more mature the past weeks.

We stopped at a hamburger joint that had tables set up outside and bought lunch. The sun was warm and the wind was cool. I felt a little more relaxed and glad to be with them. Will reached over and took Tina's hand. "Tina's coming up to school in a few weeks to root for me in the rowing matches. Isn't she?" He looked at Tina as he asked.

Tina pulled her hand away. "I don't know," she answered sharply.

Will took her hand back and *kissed it* right there in the middle of the Waco Hamburger Hole. I felt like I was watching a movie. "When the time comes, you'll know," he said with assurance. "After all, I want everyone to meet my girl."

Tina looked very cautious. "Do you think I'm your girl? Is that what you want?"

I spoke quickly with annoyance. "Obviously, that's what he thinks and that's what he wants."

Will laughed. "You tell her, Janie."

Tina smiled. "Maybe I'll be there."

I heaved a sigh of relief. "Well, that's settled."

Then the three of us laughed together. Will puffed his mouth out with a sigh. "She's a rough one to convince, but I'm not going to give up ... ever."

Tina looked frightened and happy at the same time.

We stuffed ourselves on chiliburgers, and French fries, and malts so thick you could hardly put a straw in them. We didn't talk much while we ate, just enjoyed the junk food, the sun that was getting hotter, the whiffs of spring, and the being together.

When we had finished, Will wiped his mouth and said, "Listen, I promised Peter I'd come over and look at the boat he's been working on at the dock." He turned to me. "I don't think you want to come along, right?"

"No, No, I don't want to come. But since when is Peter working at the dock?"

Will looked at me strangely from under his shaggy eyebrows. "He's got the sailing bug. He crews for a guy with a beautiful sailboat, and keeps it in condition for him. In exchange the owner is going to let him take it out sometimes."

"Oh?" I said.

Will stood up. "Janie, Peter is a growing and complicated man. There are a lot of things he wants to do. Places he wants to go. Didn't he ever talk about it with you?"

I felt annoyed at Will. He had known Peter

a few weeks and *he* was telling *me* about Peter? Peter, whom I'd known all my life. Who knew him better, Will or I? I thought it funny, too, calling Peter a man. Peter was still a boy. Duke was a man. Could anyone compare the two?

Will dropped Tina and me at the shopping center and we browsed through some stores while he went over to see Peter. He picked us up an hour later, looking excited.

"What a boat! Peter is crewing in the races next month. I'd give anything to be doing that."

Tina asked, "Can't you?"

Will shrugged. "To tell you the truth, I'm not good enough. Peter is a natural. I'm not. He's really taken to it like a pro."

I thought about that. But I couldn't picture Peter doing whatever you do on a sailboat. It just wasn't Peter.

That night my parents were going out, and I was anxious to be by myself and just think about the next day. I was pretending to read in the living room when they came downstairs. My mother looked at me in that "mother" way, peering and examining.

"You look funny," she said. "Do you feel all right?"

"I'm fine. Go and enjoy."

"You look like you have a fever. Your eyes are glazed."

She came over to me and put the back of

her hand on my forehead. "You don't feel warm."

"I'm fine, Mother. Fine!" My voice was getting shrill and I tried to keep it under control.

"I always know when my children are sick. And you seem sick."

"Mother, I'm healthy, like anything. Look, I'll do sit-ups to prove it."

My mother smiled. "Anyone who does sit-ups *has* to be sick. Well, okay. There's spaghetti and meatballs in the refrigerator for your dinner. Leftovers, but good. Just heat it all up."

I pushed her toward the door where my father was waiting patiently. *"Good night,"* I said.

I tried to concentrate on something besides Duke that night. I tried to read, watch TV, knit, even do homework, but it was all useless. At nine o'clock I went to bed, not knowing what else to do. I spent the night turning from side to side, and then sleeping for a while. I would wake up burning up and throw off the covers, fall asleep, and then wake up shivering. I thought maybe my mother was right and I had a fever. I put my hand on my forehead, as she had done, but it was cool. So I pulled up the covers and huddled under them.

I thought about what I'd say when I saw Duke. "Hi, I'm Janie Downs."

That's brilliant, I thought. *He knows you're Janie Downs.*

145

Then I said, "Hi, you must be Duke McCoy."

One thing's certain, he's not going to be attracted to you for your clever conversation, I thought.

"Hi . . ."

"Oh, Janie, for heaven's sake go to sleep!" I said out loud.

I had no idea why I suddenly was crying. I felt so alone, and so wonderfully high and so terribly low all at once, and I just wanted it to be tomorrow. And, strangely, I wanted my mother.

CHAPTER XVI_____

Even when you think tomorrow will never come, it does. When Tina and I were finally on the train to New York, I was light-headed with anticipation. I sat very quietly in my seat and Tina read a book. I looked out of the train window at the houses, and bushes, and towns slipping by. Then I looked at my own reflection in the train window. I stared at the girl appraisingly and then I looked again. "No!" I yelled.

People all over the train turned to look at me. Tina jumped and asked, "What's wrong with you?"

"Look at her," I cried, pointing to the window.

Tina looked at the window. "Look at who?"

I grabbed Tina's arm. "Look at *me*."

"You look fine. A little tired, but it makes you seem dramatic."

"Tina, I forgot. I forgot! I'm supposed to look like the picture I sent him. I don't look like that at all."

Tina gasped. "Oh, Janie. I forgot, too." She patted my arm. "It's okay, though, you look very pretty."

I pushed her hand away. "Very pretty and how old?" I asked.

"Do you want the truth or a small, harmless lie?"

I didn't answer for a moment, then I did. "The truth."

Tina shrugged slightly. "You look like sixteen . . . give or take a few months."

"Tina, what am I going to do? Can you fix my hair? Please try. Make it look like Kathy did."

Tina shook her head helplessly. "Janie, I'd do anything to help you, but I'm hopeless with hair. Why do you think I keep mine so short? I'm just no good with hair. Anyway, we don't have the pins or the combs."

I was getting desperate. "Makeup! You must have some makeup. All I have on is lipstick and a little powder. What have you got in your pocketbook?"

Tina opened her bag and began searching. "All I have is lipstick."

I started to cry. Right there in the train, like a two-year-old, I cried. Tina grabbed a tissue out of her bag and mopped at my face frantically. "Stop it," she ordered firmly.

"Stop it. Your eyes will get all red and swollen, and that will just make matters worse."

That stopped the tears quickly. I slumped in the seat and just stared out of the window. Then I turned back to Tina. "I don't even have on sophisticated clothes. I look like a baby."

I had on a flowered print cotton skirt and a white shirt. I was neat. The Girl Scouts would have loved me.

"Well, you're neat," Tina said.

"I hate you," I answered.

"And clean," she added. "And you certainly don't smell from horses, which should be a relief to him."

"I hate you," I repeated.

"Janie," Tina said. "There's nothing you can do now. You're pretty, very pretty. Prettier than any girl he's probably ever seen."

"Yeah," I mumbled, "and I look like sixteen . . . if I'm lucky."

When we got out of the train station and onto the street, it had turned into one of those hot, pre-summer days that hits New York suddenly. The sun was glaring and a veil of humidity hung over everything, making hair and clothes and spirits wilt. As we walked the blocks up to the bus terminal, I felt trickles of perspiration running down my back. "Now I'm going to smell, too," I mumbled.

Tina knew what I meant. "Well, as I said, at least it won't be from horses."

We got to the bus station with just enough time to stop at the information line and find out what gate Duke's bus was coming in on and then fight our way to it. The terminal was filled with families frantically trying to keep track of straying children; kids with huge camping packs on their backs, looking tired; and mobs of people looking confused. On the benches along the wall, there were a few drunks fast asleep, lying in dirty, torn clothes, and there were scattered bag ladies busily going through their garbage-filled shopping bags. Near the gate where Duke's bus was to arrive were two girls wearing too much makeup, high heels, and short, tight skirts.

I leaned against the wall next to the gate door and wiped the sweat off my face. "You look so pale," Tina said with concern.

"You should see how pale I am *inside*. What am I going to say to him?"

Tina pushed her hair off her face. "You never had any trouble finding things to *write* about. So just pretend he's a letter."

"I think I'm going to faint," I whispered.

"No, you're not. You're not the fainting type."

At that moment I looked out of the window in the wall that separated the waiting room from the bus ramp and saw a bus turn into the driveway and move over to the gate we were at. I barely took a breath as the bus stopped and slowly, slowly, people began to get out. Some stopped at the side for their luggage and some came right into the waiting room. I strained against the window, looking for Duke. And then I saw him. Way before he saw me. Because I couldn't believe it, I narrowed my eyes and looked at him again. "He's old!" I cried to Tina. "He's at least twenty-six or seven!"

And he was. He was also very thin. His face was weary, as if he hadn't slept in a few nights, and his clothes were wrinkled and dusty. His skin was sunburned but had a leathery look. His cowboy hat was on the back of his head but it was worn and faded by the sun. *This* was the man I had dreamed about? The man who had been the epitome of every romantic fantasy I'd ever had. I wanted to turn and run away, but he saw me as he came into the waiting room. At first he smiled broadly, and then the smile faded away and astonishment took its place. He walked over to me and looked down at me. (He was tall at least.)

"You're a kid," he shouted. "You're just a kid."

"And what about you?" I shouted back. "You're old . . . very old!"

"How old are you?" he asked. "Fifteen?"

I was really angry now. "Certainly not! I'm sixteen."

He pushed his hat farther back. "I could practically be arrested for walking out of the station with you."

I ignored him. "You. How old are *you*?"

"I'm twenty-seven. What about it?"

By this time our shouting had drawn a small group of fascinated bystanders around us, listening to every word. Tina tried to calm us down but it was useless.

"How could you do this to me?" I said breathlessly. "How could you lie to me?"

One of the made-up, high-heeled girls who was part of our little group, shook her head angrily and said, "You tell him, honey. *Men*."

"How could *I* lie?" Duke asked. "What about you? I've traveled two and a half days on a crummy bus, without hardly sleeping. For what?"

A surly-looking man in the group of observers yelled to Duke, "You tell her, buddy. Don't let her get away with anything."

Tina grabbed each of our arms. "You've got to stop this. We'll all be arrested for disturbing the peace. Please, there's a little restaurant around the corner I've been to with my mother. Let's all go there and talk quietly."

Duke shook his head in agreement. "Okay. You're right. Let's go."

"Not me," I shouted at him. "I'm not going anywhere with you!"

A bus terminal security guard came over to me and glared at Duke. "Miss, is this man bothering you?"

That snapped me back to reality. I hated Duke, but I certainly didn't want him to get into any trouble when he'd just gotten off the bus. "No. No. It's all right. I know him."

"Oh," the guard smiled knowingly. "Just a lovers' quarrel." And he walked away.

Tina, Duke, and I left the terminal in silence, and Tina led the way to a restaurant a block away. The waitress came over as soon as we sat down and gave us menus. "I need a beer," Duke said wearily.

"I'll have one, too," I added with what I hoped was assurance.

"You? Like hell," Duke said. "Have you ever had a beer?"

"I've tasted it once or twice. I'm not a child, you know."

"Yeah?" Duke asked. "Okay, what does everyone want to eat?"

"I don't want anything," I said petutantly.

Duke turned to the waitress. "Hamburgers all around. Two Cokes and one beer."

I looked at him while he ordered; then we just glared at each other. I remembered the dreams of him kissing me and how I'd been dizzy with the thought of it. I remembered running to the post office, looking for mail, and the thrill when there was a letter. All the hopes and expectations I'd had flooded me, and my disappointment was so overwhelming, my feelings of loss so monumental, that the tears started rolling down my cheeks. I had cried so much these last months that I was almost used to it, but to cry in a restaurant, in front of a strange man, was humiliating.

I tried to brush the tears away but they just kept coming and coming. "I'm sorry," I groaned. "I'm so sorry. I know I'm embarrassing you. It's just . . . it's just . . ."

Duke reached over and put a handkerchief in my hand. He patted my arm and murmured, "Don't cry, Janie. It's okay. Don't cry."

I looked up at him and there was so much kindness in his face, along with so much sadness. "Why did you do it?" he asked softly.

Tina pushed a glass of water in front of me. I took a few sips and stopped crying. "I don't know. I was bored and restless and then I saw your ad. I wanted something exciting to happen to me and you seemed to be it."

I looked directly into his eyes. "I'm sixteen. I don't go to college and I'm not a writer. I only come to town once a month and then it's with Tina. I don't go to fancy restaurants or discos or theaters. And Kathy fixed me up to look like I did in the picture I sent you."

"Who's Kathy?" Duke asked.

"She's a friend," I mumbled, and I could feel tears pushing at my eyes again.

Duke smiled at me. I knew what he was thinking. He saw me as a pathetic child. And maybe he was right.

"Well, tell Kathy she did a good job."

Then I realized *I'd* lied, but so had *he.* "Why did *you* do it?" I asked him.

Duke sat back in his chair and he drifted far away.

"I was lonely and felt my life was so ordinary. That I'd never get to do or see anything exciting. My boss' wife had a copy of *East Coast* and I saw the ads. I put one in, and then you answered."

He shrugged and laughed with embarrassment. "I sent you a picture taken six years ago. It's kind of funny. I sent you a picture of what I used to look like and you sent me one of what you're gonna look like. I guess they weren't total lies. I mean they were all us."

The waitress brought our food and after Tina had taken a bite of her hamburger she asked Duke, "Are you really a cowboy who drifts, like you said?"

"Sure, that was all true. I couldn't make that up. It's all I know. That's why I needed Janie. Roaming like I do, from place to place, I never got attached to one girl. Maybe my ma is right. Maybe I just don't want to grow up and settle down."

Duke reached over and took my hand. "Janie, we made each other up. I wanted a sophisticated city girl I could carry with me from ranch to ranch, just by taking her letters along with me. You wanted a guy who was different from the kids you know. Someone you thought was exciting. Hell, Janie, I'm not exciting."

I leaned my elbow on the table and put my head on my hand. "I feel so guilty, Duke. You came all the way from Wyoming and all there is is me."

Duke looked around the restaurant. "Listen, I'm here in New York, a place I

155

thought I'd never see. I took the bus because I wanted to see the country, and I saw it. I'm ahead, kid."

Tina was looking at Duke with real admiration. "What are you going to do the rest of the week?"

"I'll be in the rodeo. I know a lot of guys in it and we'll bum around the city. See it all. It'll be great."

"And then?" I asked.

"And then," Duke smiled wistfully, "I'll go back home and I'll try to find a girl with a little of Janie in her, but older. If I'm lucky I'll finally settle down and make a home for myself. It's time."

"You don't hate me?" I asked him.

"Do you hate me?" he asked back.

"No," I whispered, and I meant it.

"That goes double," he said.

We had finished lunch and then there was really nothing more either of us had to say to each other. After all the letters, and all the dreaming and yearning, we sat in silence.

"Well," Duke said, "I guess I'd better go."

"Duke, come home to dinner with me. My parents would like to meet you, I know."

Duke shook his head. "I don't think so, Janie. I'm going to go to my hotel, find some of the guys, and take a look at this town."

I took a piece of paper out of my bag and wrote my phone number on it. "You can call me and maybe come out some other time."

"Sure. Maybe I'll just do that."

We left the restaurant, and Tina and I told

Duke how to get to his hotel. I stood on the hot sidewalk, feeling as if I'd lost something important and not knowing exactly what. Duke set his hat on his head and put his hands on my shoulders.

"So long, Janie dear." He bent his head and very, very softly kissed me on my mouth. It was almost a dream kiss, it was so brief and so light. Then he walked away. I watched him all the way down the block, and I knew I would never see him or hear from him again as long as I lived.

I turned to Tina and said sadly, "I want to go home."

On the train I felt so tired that I put my head on Tina's shoulder and closed my eyes. I felt her sigh and then she said, "Well, he was a very nice man, anyway."

I lifted my head and looked out of the window. "Yes. Very nice, but not the man I had dreamed of. It's not his fault."

Tina agreed. "Of course it's not his fault. You made up the dream man, Janie. He helped a little, but you . . ."

"I know, Tina. I know." I turned to her. "I'm going to tell my parents about today, when I get home. Will you come with me?"

Tina shook her head. "Sure, if you think it will help."

I smiled a half smile. "I don't know what will help, but it can't hurt."

I told my parents the whole story. When I started with "I met Duke today," my father looked furious and my mother terrified. But when I finished the whole pitiful tale, they both looked wistful. My father stood up and filled his pipe. He always does that when he's stalling for time. "Well," he said, "he sounds like a nice young man."

"Only not so young," I added a little angry.

"Not exactly ready to turn in his horse either," my father said defensively.

My mother put her arms around me and I knew she was ready for a long, analytical heart-to-heart. I gently disengaged myself from her embrace. "Mom, please don't say anything. I have to figure out how I got to this place and why. And I have to do it alone."

CHAPTER XVII‗‗‗‗‗‗

And that's what I started to do.

I went to school every day and I ate lunch with Kathy and Tina, but after school I went home by myself. They both tried to be with me, and I knew they wanted to talk to me about Duke, but I couldn't. I took long walks, alone. I went on long bike rides, alone. At night sometimes I'd watch a little TV with my parents and then I'd go up to my room and look out of the window at the millions of stars. Even weekends I stayed away from the kids. I had to get to know *me* a little better and I couldn't do it in a crowd.

I cried a lot, too, as silently as I could. I felt so lost. Little by little, I was able to pick up some of the pieces of the Janie puzzle and line them up so I could look at them and see what shape they were. I realized that I had always been a dreamer. That's not all bad, but it's not all good either. Somehow, my dream life always seemed more interesting than my real life. While other girls were joining clubs and teams, and planning their futures, I was making up little dramatic stories in which I was the star. I know most girls do that, and probably boys, too, but I went a little further, so that it had been so easy to make up Duke, too. Duke was a nice man, and a cowboy was certainly different, and he *had* lied about his age, but he'd never pretended to be a hero in a movie. He'd never pretended to be glamorous or anything exotic. I'd given him that role. He probably didn't even kiss so good either.

I was beginning to have some idea of what had been happening to me. But how was I going to change? You don't just snap your fingers, say "reality," and stop years of what had been very nice, superior daydreaming.

One day after school, during the second week after I'd seen Duke, I rode my bike out to the Point, thinking about this new problem. It was a beautiful May day, the kind that made you want to just lie on the grass somewhere and sniff the air. It was a long ride, and when I got there I stopped on a walk above the docks and looked at the boats and the sky and the birds swooping down to the blue water. I watched a man working on one of the large sailboats. He had on cutoff jeans and no shirt. His legs were firm and long. His back was already tanned from the sun and I watched the muscles moving smoothly under his tight skin. *Good-looking*, I thought. And then, *I guess I'm getting*

better, if I can feel a man is that attractive.
A hopeful sign.

Suddenly, the man raised his head and looked up at me. It was Peter. I was startled and amazed. We looked at each other for a long moment, neither of us moving. Then I turned, quickly pushed my bike up the walk, and rode off. *Peter.* I had responded to someone I had thought was a *man,* and it had been *Peter.* I pedaled automatically, going faster and faster. I tried not to think about whether my heart was beating so fast from the exercises or from the way Peter had looked to me.

I went up to my room very early that night and I took out the old picture of Peter I had put away. I looked at it carefully, put it back in the drawer, and went over to my window. I knelt on the floor and rested my head on my arms on the window sill and looked out at the familiar street. I thought about how many times Peter had come up that street to my house. And I remembered other things. I heard Will's voice saying, "Peter is a complicated man." Will had said *man,* plain as anything.

"There are a lot of things he wants to do," Will had said. "Didn't he ever talk about them with you?"

No. He hadn't. Why? Peter certainly wasn't shy. Was it my fault? Had I ever been interested? Ever asked? Or had I just been little girl Janie, wanting to be amused, and gently kissed, and cared for?

I remembered the day the year before,

when Peter and I had been listening to records in the den and my mother had cut her finger very badly. Peter had run into the kitchen when he heard her cry out and I had followed. Mother was standing at the sink with blood gushing out of a deep cut. He had looked at her wound and then her pale face, had wrapped a clean towel around her finger, and carefully had led her out to the car.

"Where are you going?" I had asked shakily.

"I'm taking her to the doctor. You stay here."

He'd brought her back in an hour. Her finger had been stitched and she looked whiter than before. I stayed with her while she lay down, and Peter had made dinner. No fuss, he'd just cooked the whole meal, quietly and competently. It wasn't bad either, if you like olives in soup, which Peter does.

I remembered the day his dog had been run over when Peter was sixteen. He'd held the dead dog in his lap in the street and he'd let the tears run down his cheeks, not caring about the stupes that thought a grown boy shouldn't cry.

As I got ready for bed, I was aware of unfamiliar, new feelings for Peter. Was I just a flighty, fickle girl who careened from one boy, man, to another? Was I the kind of girl who *had* to have a boy to think about? Who wasn't complete without at least a dream of a boy?

All the rest of that week in school, I could

sense in my pores when Peter was nearby. I watched him carefully, examining my feelings. I saw things that must have *always* been there, but I'd never been aware of. A funny, half-smile that came and went very quickly, when he did something well, like smack the ball over the net into the perfect spot in a tight game of tennis. In the cafeteria, I saw him sitting with a group of boys who were part of the debating team, and I saw Peter's look of intensity as he argued with them. How come I'd never noticed it before?

I watched the way girls turned and looked after him when he walked down the hall, the appraising glance he gave them as he went by, sometimes looking back after them. Nothing little boy about *that*. I felt a piercing stab of jealousy when I saw his head turn.

One day when I was working in the library, I looked up and saw him sitting at a table, watching me. We stared at each other and a feeling of warmth started at my toes and climbed to my face. We didn't smile. We didn't move. I looked away, confused and out of breath. But I knew clearly that I had to talk to Peter.

That Saturday there was a picnic in Bobby Argo's backyard, and I went. Peter was there, too. I was afraid to see if he'd brought Clare and tried to look around casually. Tina dumped a bag of potato chips in my lap as I stretched out on the grass.

"He's alone," she said in a low voice.

I was surprised. "How did you know I cared? I haven't said a word to anyone."

"Know?" she repeated. "You've been peering at him like he was some strange, new species of *Homo sapiens* all week."

"Oh, no! Did *everyone* notice?"

Tina reassured me. "Of course not, but when two people have been friends as long as we have, how could I not know?"

I sat up and pulled at the grass. "I feel nutsy. I mean, I feel so attracted to him and he's *Peter*. Why do you suppose this is happening to me *now*, when I've known him all my life?"

"I don't know," Tina answered. "Maybe you're ready to feel this way. Maybe you just needed some kind of jolt, like Duke, to help you 'mature,' as my mother would say."

"I don't feel very mature right now. What should I do, Tina? I want him to know how I feel."

"So tell him," Tina said.

I made a face at her and answered with annoyance, "I can't just go up to him and say, 'Peter, I think you're really something and I've been a jerk for not realizing it before.'"

"Why not?"

"I just can't. Maybe he'd just walk away and I'd die."

Tina was thoughtful for a while. "Well, you seem to excel with your little pen and paper, so write to him."

I did, though it took me a few days to gather enough courage together. But Monday night, though my hand trembled as I held my pen, I wrote:

Dear 420 Elm Street,
    I am a girl who lives at 428 Elm Street and I've been going through what the school psychologist would call "a growing experience."

I then told him the whole pitiful story about Duke, trying to be honest and not spare myself. I ended the letter saying:

    If you would like to meet an unsophisticated, small-town girl who shares many of your interests and who thinks you are . . . I'll save that for another time... please write.
                    Yours truly,
                    Love,
                    428 Elm Street

The next morning I waited until I saw Peter walking to school and I ran to his house and put the letter in his mailbox. All that day I felt like I was back to where I'd been with Duke, waiting like a fool for a letter, figuring, if he reads it at such and such an hour, and he answers it at such and such an hour, and he ... etc.
The next morning, there was a note in my

mailbox. I was so frightened at what it might say that I waited until I met Tina to open it. When I got to her house I waved the note. "I'm afraid to open it."

Tina took the letter from me. "You know, this feels very *déjà vu*." She opened the note, read it, and handed it to me. "It's not exactly the love letter of the century, but it will do very nicely."

Dear 428 Elm Street,
    You sound like a girl I used to know. If you like horror movies, too, I'll pick you up at 7:30 Friday night.
                        Love,
                        420 Elm Street

"Tina, I feel like I'm going out on my first date."

Tina patted my back. "And I won't even be here to give you instructions."

"Why not?"

Tina looked strangely shy for Tina. "I'm going up to watch Will's rowing matches on Saturday. Will's parents are going, too, and we're driving up Friday evening. It's Will's last weekend at school, so we're all coming home together."

I laughed out loud, real loud. "Great! Double Great! We're *both* having 'growing experiences.'"

Tina smiled wryly. "But why do they have to be so scary? I mean if it's so natural, why isn't it easy?"

CHAPTER XVIII _____

On Friday my mother went into the city to meet Dad for dinner. Mellie had come home from college for the summer, and at six o'clock we ignored my mother's instructions to heat the nutritious casserole that was in the refrigerator and fried hot dogs instead. While we were piling on the mustard and sauerkraut Mellie said, "How about a movie after dinner?"

I hesitated. I hadn't told anyone except Tina and Kathy about my date with Peter. I figured if it turned out to be a disaster, why should everyone in Filby know? But I didn't want to lie to Mellie. "I have a date . . . with Peter," I said.

Melanie raised her eyebrows in surprise. Mellie used her eyebrows the way other people use their eyes or mouths. If she ever shaved them off no one would be able to tell what she was feeling. I wouldn't mind being able to hide *my* feelings that easily. Now I turned away so she couldn't see how nervous I was as she asked, "How did all this come about?"

I briefly filled her in on the last few weeks and said, "How come, Mellie? How come I didn't feel this way about Peter before? I feel so stupid and shallow and childish."

Mellie seemed to be mentally going through her psych books before she answered. "I think lots of times we just take people for granted because they've been around forever. I remember the first time I looked at Mother and saw her as a *person*. I mean, not 'Mother,' but a separate woman named Fran. It was a real shocker."

I nodded, remembering the ride with my father when I looked at him as an individual for almost the first time. I was doing the same thing with Peter.

I was no longer thinking of him as "the boy next door," and was seeing him almost as a new boy in town. I certainly felt as if this was my first date with him. I put on my one pair of designer jeans, which were a soft, pale blue. I wore a purple, cowl-necked T-shirt with them, and put just a touch of light blue eyeshadow on my eyelids and pale, pale pink lipstick on my mouth. It was all just right, not overdone, but sexy, good taste. When I heard Peter banging on the door, I grabbed a sweater that matched the jeans perfectly to throw around my shoulders.

I ran downstairs and opened the door. "Hi," I said softly. "Come on in."

He looked at me, smiling slightly. I could see the expression of approval that passed over his face. "Hi, yourself. We have to go now if we want to make the eight o'clock show. It's over in Eastport."

We made small talk during the short ride to the theater. I could tell that Peter felt as self-conscious as I did. During the movie, I was only dimly aware of the monster on the screen. It was a dinosaur from the waist up and a human from the waist down. It went around snorting and knocking down buildings, when it wasn't grabbing at the heroine and eating trees. I was acutely aware of Peter's shoulder touching mine, and his knee not touching mine. When we both reached into the tub of popcorn at the same time and our fingers touched, I felt buttery shocks run up my arm. I wanted him to put his arm around me, but I knew he wasn't going to. I wondered what we would do after the movie. Go out? Go home?

I could hardly sit still in the seat, so I concentrated hard on keeping my hands and feet as immobile as possible.

After the movie I waited for Peter to suggest *something*. I was terrified that he was waiting for *me* to suggest something. But he wasn't. "Janie, why don't we go home? We've got a lot to talk about."

My heart plunged into my toes at the cool, unemotional tone of his voice. I was practically unable to put one foot in front of the other, and he sounded as if he was getting ready to work on Latin verbs.

"Sure," I said, surprised that I sounded as calm as he did. "You're right."

When we went into the den at home, I turned on all the lights so that he wouldn't think I was trying in any way to be seductive. He watched me as I turned on the fourth lamp. "What are you planning on doing? Major surgery?"

I turned off the lamp and sank down into a chair, watching as Peter paced around the room restlessly. Finally he stood still and faced me. "Were you in love with him . . . this Duke guy?"

"No," I answered quickly. "Not the way you mean. I mean, not the real Duke. He was old and dusty. Kind but not exciting. I made up the man I was writing to. He never existed the way I dreamed him. I mean, I invented this cowboy movie star and . . . I don't know if I can explain," I finally said helplessly. "I've made such a mess of things."

Peter sat down on the couch opposite me, waiting for me to go on. Go on to *what*? I wasn't sure and I was wildly uncomfortable. How honest was I supposed to be? But I plunged on. "I guess it was because you and I grew up together. I took you for granted." I sighed with embarrassment. "I didn't really *see* you. How . . . how special . . . and really wonderful . . . and all sorts of things you are. Does that hurt you a lot?"

Peter smiled a little now. "Yeah, it hurts. But I remember how I used to daydream about a model I used to see in Fenton's department store. I used to pretend . . . well, never mind."

"You *did?*"

"Yeah, but I never did anything about it. While you . . . you . . . Janie, you wrote letters and you met him."

I put my head down in my hands and said with urgency, "I'm sorry, Peter. I am. Really. I think I was a little crazy for a while."

Then I got up and sat next to him on the couch. I decided that if I was going to plunge in, I'd plunge in. I took his hand . . . and he let me. "I really care about you, Peter. More than I imagined. Can't we start over?"

I was carried away with this wonderful idea. My eyes sparkled and I grinned as I said eagerly, "Can't we pretend that we've just met? That we don't know each other and . . ."

"No, Janie! No pretending!"

I shook my head with discouragement and put it on his shoulder. "Peter, maybe I have some kind of disease. Maybe I'm an uncontrollable pretender. Maybe I'll be written about in textbooks as a rare, sad case, a trial to her parents and friends."

Peter took my face in his hands and looked deep, deep into my eyes. There was an expression in his I hadn't seen before. "Janie, love, some things are better than pretending."

He bent his head and kissed me. In all my dreams of Duke's kisses I had never felt the way I did with Peter's mouth on mine. It was all unfamiliar and wonderfully different. I was in a new place, caught up in a building sweep of response and exhilaration. I reached up and put one hand on the back of his head and the other around his neck, and he moved his hands from my face and circled his arms around me. When he lifted his mouth from my lips, we clung together.

"You've changed, Janie," he whispered.

I moved my head and looked up at him. "Is it good?" I asked, smiling and knowing the answer.

Peter jumped up from the couch and pulled me with him. He put his arms around my waist, and we spun around the room together. "Good?" he asked breathlessly. "It's great!"

Then he stopped and held me away from him. "I don't really understand all this," he said.

"I don't either, but it feels . . . right."

Peter looked at me. "I love you, Jane."

"I love you, Peter," I answered.

And I wasn't pretending.